CU00970829

Steamy Research

An Erotic Tale from Marie's

Barton, D

DMBbooks

After publishing a bunch of books, it's pretty hard to write a dedication that you haven't written before. Feeling like I can't just be thanking the same people over and over.

However, you should always thank the people who help and support you. You can never say thank you enough. So I thank my family, my gorgeous wife and my wonderful son. For any friend who has sparked an idea or helped me with a problem.

Every little thing that has kept me going on this journey is greatly appreciated. So thank you, to you all.

Contents

Chapter 1

The peace of my sleep was the only escape I got from the dull pain that filled my heart every day. The rhythmic beep hitting my ears and rippling through that darkness, disturbing me awake. Beep after beep calling me to the real world.

I opened my eyes and saw the boring white walls of the hospital. Blinking to get rid of the cobwebs that hid in the corners of my mind. I sat up in the chair that had gotten used to my sleeping posture. So much so that there was a permanent groove that cradled my back and butt perfectly. I rubbed my palms over my eyelids trying to shake off the last of my sleepiness.

Then my eyes fell on the hospital bed and that rip in my heart threatened to open like a canyon of hurt. Lying there for the better part of a year was my thirteen year old daughter. After a horrible car accident that took the life of my parents, she had ever since been in a coma. Unresponsive with a tube to feed her and an IV for fluids.

The doctors have told me time and time again that she is stable but she may never wake up. I've always replied with the same answer. They didn't know my daughter. And they didn't. She has proven to be stronger than I had ever thought a young girl could be.

My hand reached over, fingers curled around hers. Every time I touched her it surprised me how warm she was. After watching her lie there so still and quiet for so long. I kept expecting her skin to be cold. Only it was as warm as her personality.

I turned my arm over and saw that it was almost noon on my silver watch. Rubbing a hand over my face I stood from the chair. Letting the blanket fall onto the bed. Pecking my daughter's forehead before moving out the door.

Sitting almost opposite was the nurse's station. Doris was working today and she always greeted me with a huge smile, every single time. Her eyes rose to mine and she shone that big smile. No matter how bad a day I was having, it would always lift my heart. "Coffee time, Mrs Rogers?"

"Yes. Something to kick-start my body."

"Good luck with that. You know how bad the coffee is here."

"Indeed I do but it's the only option at the moment." I gave her a sleepy wave before turning and walking down the halls of the hospital. Following the yellow line to the cafeteria. I brought a cup of the tasteless muck they insulted us with by calling it coffee.

Taking a sip brought out a grimace but I swallowed it anyway, needing the caffeine. Turning back I re-traced my route along the yellow line. But before I got back to my daughter's room a large figure came running into me.

Not only did my petite body get knocked into the wall. My coffee was sent falling to the floor. It might have tasted horrible but it was something I needed right now. I looked up and saw the face of this man looking around like he had lost his child amongst a crowd.

"Watch where you're going next time." My words were filled with venom.

"Which way is it?" It seemed more of a rhetorical question than one aimed at me so I simply ignored him and made my way back to the cafeteria. I got a second cup of sludge and then walked back to my daughter's room making sure not to get it spilt this time.

As I walked in through the door I saw the doctor leaning over her. Shining his light into her eyes. "No response still?"

He looked up at me. His light brown hair a little ruffled up like he had just woken up as well. "No." It had gotten to the point where the doctors would be direct and honest. They wouldn't run around the situation with fancy medical words. I appreciated it even if it stung a little sometimes.

I sat down as he finished his inspection of my comatose daughter. Once he was done he sat on the bed, resting his hands on his lap. "How are you holding together?"

"A little tired but I'm okay. I got a shift at the library soon so I'll be out of your hair."

"You know you never get in the way. In truth I've gotten used to you being here. But maybe you should go home to sleep. Your bed must be more comfortable than that chair."

"I don't know. I've grown accustomed to it. I don't think I could fall asleep in a bed any more. Not without her down the hallway."

The doctor smiled at me before looking at her in the bed. "I best get back to my rounds. Hope work is okay for you. Like always, we'll call if there are any changes."

"Thank you, Doctor Williams." The young doctor gave me another smile before leaving the room. He had always been the friendliest one. At first I found it hard to trust someone younger than myself with the life of my daughter. Now there wasn't anyone I trusted more than him.

I drank my horrible coffee and read my book. For the first six months I never did anything but watch my daughter. The nurse had said it was my mind not wanting to miss a second.

She told me it wasn't healthy and I needed to relax. So now I brought books from work. Puzzles from the gift shop in the hospital. Something to pass the time. To keep my mind sane for when she did wake up.

Once it was time for my shift I packed up my things. Told my daughter that I loved her and left. Going straight from the hospital, up the road and into the city centre. I found the library with its red brick work and gothic designed windows. Something that wouldn't look out of place on a church.

It stood out from the more modern buildings around it. One of those rare times that something old wasn't falling apart or needing repairs. It stood just as sturdy as it did when it was first built. Or at least that's what my boss always said.

I walked through the automatic doors. Took off my grey cardigan and rolled it around my handbag. Tucking the bundle under the desk I sat down and logged into the computer. Five minutes later my boss arrived from the storage room upstairs.

Wearing his usual grey polo shirt and black trousers. Fluffy grey hairs stuck out with his shiny head poking through the middle. He was always friendly and cheery. Happy to give me the part time job so I could spend most my time with my daughter.

When he came to the desk it was the usual questions of how I was doing? How was my daughter? And I gave the same answers I always provided. It had become part of my working day routine. I knew he really didn't want the complicated answers just as he knew I didn't want to give them.

The rest of my work day was standard for a Saturday. A few customers came in who needed help. I read books from the shelves and then I clocked out. No call from the hospital to say that my daughter had made a miraculous recovery. So I took a slow walk through the city. Watching shops shutting up and locking their shutters.

I thought about taking the doctor's advice and heading home but then I saw a road sign. That big H symbol standing out in red like it could read my mind. Telling me to return. I wasn't one for looking out for signs from the universe so it must have been the lack of sleep that persuaded me to return.

The night shift nurse was on when I got back onto the ward. Unlike the day shift, the nurses who worked the unsocial hours weren't as cheerful. They looked like zombies in blue uniforms. But I caught Doctor Williams on his way out with his motorcycle helmet. "Back?"

"You know I can't stay away."

His smile increased, "I'll see you tomorrow then. If you're asleep I'll make sure I don't wake you when I do my checks."

"Don't worry about that." His hand came up and rubbed my shoulder reassuringly. I found myself thinking if he was eleven years older I'd take him home with me. What else would a thirty-five year old do with someone so cute?

I stopped off at the cafeteria to pick up some sludge as I yawned. Walking around the corner for the second time today a body came crashing against my walk. The cup slipped from my fingertips and I couldn't help but watch it bounce onto the floor. "For fuck sake." Looking up I saw the same man from before. Only this time he didn't look as lost. Seeing bloodshot eyes and the stains of tears on his cheeks. "You again."

"Oh god. I'm sorry. Look, here, have mine."

He offered his cup to me and I took it slowly. "Thanks."

"Although I don't think it's such a favour since it tastes so horrible."

"Yeah." I looked up at him more closely. Seeing the glazed look in his eyes. The way he wasn't really focused on me despite his words being directed at me. "I know this is a stupid question because I've been asked it so many times before. But, are you okay?"

His eyes met mine and they seemed to see me for the first time. Not surprising he had bumped into me twice. "Um..no."

"Stupid, I know."

He suddenly burst out a brief laugh before seeming to catch himself. "Yes but what else are you supposed to ask?"

"Very true." Now I was smiling. "I've been here almost a year now, so if you need to talk to someone about it. Just come find me."

"Well." He looked over his shoulder like he was looking for permission before he asked, "How about I take you for something we can call coffee?" His fingers plucked the cup from my hands. "It would be a true way to apologise for knocking into you twice."

"I really should go see my daughter."

"Right. Yes. Sorry for asking."

"No, no. It's okay." I saw the pain in his eyes and I knew exactly how that felt. I wanted to go see my daughter because it's been set that if I was there when the visiting hours finished, they just let me stay all night.

I had done that for what seemed like an age now. But something deep down inside me told me to agree. "How about I meet you out the front in a half hour? We'll go grab that coffee."

"Sounds good." He thanked me before walking off to take a seat in the cafeteria. My feet took me to my daughter who I kissed and chatted to for a little bit. I told her about work like I used to when she was awake.

Once she was filled in and I told her I loved her. She received a hug and I left the room. Waving to the night nurse I made my way to the front. Not spotting the guy in the cafeteria I assumed he had changed his mind.

Getting outside I peered over the road to see him smoking a cigarette. He was cowering underneath a tree branch to keep his suit out of the rain. Quickly running across when it was clear I joined him under that branch. "Hey, thanks for waiting."

"Thank you for agreeing to grab a coffee. Are we walking or driving?"

"I don't have a car. Do you live here?"

"I do."

"Have you heard of Carl's café? It's in walking distance."

"I haven't. Let's pop to my car. I have an umbrella in the back."

"Sure." The man took one last drag on his cigarette and pushed it into the fag bin. He took me into the car park where we walked up to the back of a sports car. My jaw dropped open when I saw it. "This is yours?"

"It is. I know it's not the most practical way to come to the hospital but it was what I was out in when

I got the call." The boot was opened and he pulled out a long, black umbrella. Popping it open it covered the space above us easily. I scooted a little closer to make sure I didn't get any wetter.

He locked his car and we walked together to the café I had mentioned. There wasn't much talking as we made our way. The general chat about the weather and such. When we got there he went up to the counter after getting my coffee preferences.

He came back with two large, round cups that were steaming with heat. I grabbed a few packets of sugar and stirred them in with a wooden stick. Sipping at the hot edge of my mug I sighed as the true taste of coffee trickled down my throat. It heated me up from the walk and soothed my soul.

The man looked at me as I drank. His eyes darted away when my eyes lifted to his. "I have a daughter at the hospital."

"Huh?" He looked back at me with a surprised look.

"I figured I would get the awkward parts out the way first. My daughter is in a coma for ten months. Car accident, she was with my parents."

"Are they at the hospital as well?"

"No." I blinked as my eyes built with tears. "They died at the scene." I took another sip of my coffee to distract my thoughts.

"I suppose it's my turn."

"That's the idea." I watched his eyes as he thought about what to tell me.

"My..... sister is in critical care. She got mugged.

The man didn't like the lack of money she had so he stabbed her, three times."

"Oh, I'm sorry." Somehow his story sounded worse than mine. The violent nature of it making my story seem so small.

The corners of his mouth curled up as he looked at me. Then his eyes moved down to the coffee in front of him. His thumb ran around the rim of his mug. "I wasn't there with her."

"You would be in the hospital next to her if you were. Don't beat yourself up about it."

"You don't understand."

"I do. How many times do you think I thought to myself that I should have been driving? If I hadn't been at work it would have been me. Maybe I would have taken a different route. Or drove slower or faster. Just a few seconds either way and my daughter wouldn't be in a coma." I was unable to stop the tear running along the bottom of my eye before trickling down the side of my nose. I quickly rubbed it away and cleared my throat. "So don't beat yourself up about it."

The man didn't reply. He simply smiled and stood up from his chair. "Right. I'm going to go to the bathroom. I will rub my eyes maybe get a few more tears out of my system and when I come back we will talk about much happier things."

"Deal." I raised my mug up to say cheers to the idea and took another sip. Watching him walk off I followed his figure. His suit looked just as expensive as his car. I wondered what he did for a living.

He was gone for a few minutes when music

came blaring out of his phone. It had been left on the corner of the table. Flashing on the screen behind the name was a picture of a blonde woman. Her name was Nikki and the music kept going like she knew he would pick up eventually.

The device went quiet just before the man came back. "You're phone was just going off. Your wife?"

His eyebrows creased in the middle as he frowned. The phone was picked up and the number inspected. "No, that's just a friend. It won't be anything important."

"You sure. I don't mind taking a rain check." Half of my coffee had disappeared already and if I was quick I could run back and make it in time to sleep the night at the hospital.

"No, no. It's okay. Nothing important. Tell me, what do you do for work?"

"I thought we were going to talk about happier things and you're bringing up work?"

He laughed which seemed to make his green eyes twinkle. "That is a good point but I couldn't think of anything else to ask you." The man smiled at me with a sense of shyness.

"Okay then. I work at the library. Haven't been there for that long. Maybe eight months. But I love books and they let me take as many as I like as long as I bring them back."

"Sounds good for a book lover."

"That's me." Now this time I smiled and it was a strange feeling to be happy. An emotion that wasn't in my heart very much lately. Maybe it was just nice to have an adult conversation with someone other than a nurse or a doctor. There was my room mate but we barely saw each other between her working and me being at the hospital. "What about you? What allows you to afford such a nice car and clothes?"

"You noticed, huh?" That smile curling his lips again. Thinking how handsome he was. "I'm self-employed actually. Make my own hours and when I work hard I do get quite a bit of money for it."

"Hence the flashy sports car."

The man nodded. "Hence the flashy sports car."

"So, what do you do exactly?"

"I'm an author." I couldn't help but feel the little skip in my book lover's heart. He must have seen the expression on my face because he smiled wide. "I guess we're a match made in heaven. One person who writes books and the other who loves to read them."

"I guess so. So, would I have read any of them?"

"Well it all depends on how much time you spend reading erotica."

I could feel my cheeks flushing red. Adverting my eyes, slowly shaking my head. "I don't really read that kind of thing."

"Oh?" His eyebrows rose in fake shock. "Is that so?"

Looking up I couldn't hide the fact I was lying, like he could see it in my eyes. He no doubt saw the embarrassment I felt in my cheeks. "Maybe I do. You don't see many male authors in that genre."

"Hence why I don't use my real name. I write under a woman's name. My agent said that the kind of books I write, would sell better that way."

"I can understand that. If a woman sees a guy's name on an erotica book, she's probably thinking it's just about tits and arse."

The man suddenly chuckled, rubbing his fingers across that stubbled chin. "Tits and arse, huh? Well no critics have ever said that about my books."

"I'm sure. So which ones have you written?"

"There are quite a few out there. But my most successful is the trilogy I trying to finish. The first two are The Bet and The Debt."

"And the third?"

"Well, you'll just have to wait for it to be released."

"That gives me enough time to read the first two then."

"Exactly." We both laughed and it was so easy to forget my real life. Easy to slip into the thought that this was a date. Eyes running over his face again. Taking in that dark hair, swept to the side. Nice and neat just like the rest of his appearance. "I find writing them the easy part. However, I get lost in the research for my stories."

"Research for an erotic novel? I bet you could get lost in that for years."

"My job does have its perks." Again he smiled but this time it was more than before. His eyes adding to the intensity of it as he looked into mine. "Just like yours."

"Not exactly the same."

"I should hope not. Would be a hell of a library

to visit."

"I don't think many members would be interested in the books."

"Not with you working there." It sounded like a compliment but it was said with such casualness that it was easy to dismiss.

I drank my coffee as his phone blared out that ringtone again. His eyes dipped down to the screen but that smile vanished as he saw the number. It was answered quickly and the look he had got worse as I heard the mumbled voice at the other end. "Okay, I'll be right there." The man shot up out of the chair and pulled on his jacket. "I have to get back to the hospital."

"Oh."

I started to get up but he held his hand out to stop me. "I'd rather go back by myself." That look he had told me it was bad news and not the kind that would go away by the end of the day. So I sat back down. "Keep the umbrella. I'll grab it off of you next time."

"Next time?"

He pulled a smile but the sadness he felt dampened the way it looked. Giving me a gentle nod as he slipped his jacket on. "Louise."

A simple smile was returned in reply. "Matt." My head turned as he jogged out of the café and into the rain that had worsened. Checking my watch I knew I wouldn't get back before visiting hours were over so I finished my coffee and headed to the bus stop.

Climbing up and swiping my yearly pass. The

trip was short before I arrived back at the apartment building. My legs started feeling tired halfway up the stairs. Finally getting up to the one bedroom home I let myself in with the spare key.

The soft music that could be heard hit me once I opened the door. I took my coat off and hung it up on the hook with the burrowed umbrella. Turning left I placed my keys, card holder and my phone in the bowl that sat on the brown table. Making sure my ringtone was all the way up.

My shoes were put into the racking and I padded my way into the apartment. I checked the bathroom but my room mate wasn't there. "Kelly!" She didn't hear me over the music so I kept checking around. The lounge and the kitchen were one big room and she wasn't there either.

The only place left was her bedroom. But as I drew closer to the slightly ajar door there were more noises, heavy breathing. She must be doing some exercises. "Kelly!"

There was a pause in the breathing then a couple of thuds followed. I stood there waiting for a response. I only got one once the music was switched off. "Louise?"

"Yeah. Sorry if I interrupted you exercising." The door was pulled open but it wasn't Kelly standing there.

My whole body frozen as a young man came running out, buttoning up his jeans. A t-shirt flung over his shoulder showing off his toned body. He gave me a sheepish look before dodging around me and exiting the apartment.

Shocked I walked into her room where she was laying under a sheet. A sly grin shining through as she spoke out of breath. "Hey there, roomy."

"Hey, Kelly. I'm sorry for interrupting you with......who was that? He looked young enough to be my son."

"He's not that young."

"Another one of your students?"

"Which makes him at least 18." A finger was pointed at me. "That's old enough."

I couldn't help but laugh. "You're going to get into trouble with their parents one of these days."

"Only if they tell them and I doubt they will." She slid out of her bed, pulling the sheet around her like a makeshift robe. I walked out of the room as she shuffled after me. "How come you're back tonight? Haven't seen you for days."

"I missed the cut off for visitors."

"Really? How did that happen?"

"I grabbed a coffee with a guy."

Her face went from shocked to happy and she started giggling like we were back in school. "Oh really? And what was he like? Tall? Handsome?"

"Well I know he's old enough." She burst out laughing as I giggled.

"You dirty girl."

"Hold on. Nothing happened. He was at the hospital to see his sister. She was stabbed during a mugging."

"Oh." She looked ashamed of her comments but

that smile still lingered.

"Yeah. So I asked him to get a coffee so he could talk. Honestly it was nice to chat with someone. Another adult."

"You could chat with me." She tugged the corner of her sheet inside her freshly made sheet gown and poured herself a glass of water. She offered me one and I took it. "So, are you going to see this guy again?"

"Well I have his umbrella." Nodding over to the thing hanging by my coat.

"So that's a yes."

"He got some bad news and had to run back to the hospital. I don't know if he'll be in the right mood for another chat."

"Or you'll find that he'll be more up for it. Something to distract him. Distract you as well." My eyes met hers. Kelly gave me a smile which quickly faded. "How is she doing?"

That question bringing that pain in my chest. "No change."

"No news can be good news."

"I know." Sipping my water. "Thanks" I smiled but even she knew it wasn't from happiness. It was just habit. "Anyway, I'm feeling tired."

"No. This is the first night I've had you home in far too long. We are going to eat ice cream and watch silly movies."

This time when I smiled it was genuine. Kelly's care-free personality lightened my mood. "Sure. I'll get the ice cream, you pick the movies."

"Deal." She jogged off into her room to get some of her favourite films and to hopefully put on some clothes. I raided the freezer for a tub of ice cream to share and two spoons from the drawer. Kelly came back out wearing a black vest top and a pair of shorts. Tying her black hair into a ponytail. "We've only got cookie dough."

"That's the best flavour." I dropped myself onto the sofa whilst she put on the first movie. Typically it was the usual romcom that she always put on. Tonight I managed to get through five mouthfuls of ice cream and fifteen minutes of the movie before I fell asleep at one end of the sofa.

Chapter 2

When I awoke I found the blanket I usually slept under covering me. I pushed it off and looked over to see Kelly dancing to some pop music in the kitchen. I groaned as I tried to sit up. My body was used to the chair, not the sofa.

Swinging my legs over the edge I rubbed a palm over my face. Kelly noticed me as I walked over to the kitchen counter. "Hey, have a nice night?" She winked at me and I responded by slapping her arm. "Touchy. Breakfast?"

"Yes, please. I'm just going to get changed."

"Sure." I walked back over to the sofa and leaned over the back. Grabbing some clean underwear, a black shirt and some black jeans from my bag. Kelly lived in a single bed apartment so the living room was essentially my bedroom. Entering the bathroom I took off the old clothing from the day before and chucked them into the clothes basket.

I looked at myself in the mirror. The face that stared back looked awful. Touching my fingertips to my skin, pulling it and stretching it out. I could do with a shower to revitalise my body.

So I hopped into the cubicle. Enjoyed the

feeling of the water washing away all the grogginess and the grime I could feel in my pores. I washed my long brunette hair, running my fingers from root to tip slowly. And the last five minutes I just stood there with the water cascading over my figure.

Kelly called me to say the breakfast was ready so I jumped out, dried my body with a nice fluffy towel and got dressed. I walked out and she had two plates set up on the counter that split the kitchen from the lounge.

I grabbed a stool from the corner and sat opposite her. Asking her, "So what are you doing to do today?"

"Work then back here. Should I expect you tonight?"

Our eyes met over the ketchup bottle between us. "If I do come back will I be seeing another one of your students running out of the apartment?"

"Well you could join in." She gave me a cheeky grin and wink and I couldn't stop the laugh that burst out.

"I plan on sleeping at the hospital. It just felt wrong not being there."

"Okay. I'll set some homework for one of my students then."

"You are terrible. Do you ask them to call you professor in the bedroom?"

"The best ones don't need asking."

"And the rest?"

"Just need a little guidance. What about you? Going to see that guy again?"

"I do need to return his umbrella. Maybe I'll keep an eye out for him."

"You should take him out. He no doubt needs it. You could do with a night out as well."

I finished my sausage before answering. "Doesn't a night of movies count?"

"It might if you hadn't fallen asleep." She got a piece of bacon flicked at her. "Trust me. You need to go and have fun and maybe even get a guy into bed."

"Or sofa." Kelly had been nice enough to let me stay here and she knew I appreciated it. She knew it wasn't spoken in a bad way.

"Go to his. That way you can have an amazing night and disappear."

"That's your scene, not mine."

"How long has it been?"

"I'm not interested in just sex."

Kelly rolled her eyes. "Answer the question."

As I scooped up a spoonful of beans I contemplated flinging it at her but I was too hungry. Eating it I smiled at her. "You know how long it's been."

"That's what I thought. You need some sex. A good seeing to. A nice big cock stuffed inside…"

"Okay, that's enough. I think you need to cut yourself down. It seems to be going to your head."

"I know where it goes. Trust me." She finished her breakfast, put the plate in the sink and disappeared into her room. By the time I finished mine she had re-emerged looking much older than she acts.

Wearing a blue skirt with a matching jacket

and a white blouse. She reminded me of the teachers I used to have when I went to college. And the guys seemed to like her like that. Otherwise they wouldn't keep coming back here.

She left me in the apartment. I tidied up, washed up the plates and the cutlery. Tossed on my coat and my black boots before heading out. Carrying the umbrella under my arm. Pockets filled with my phone, keys and cards.

Using my bus pass, getting off just up from the hospital. I grabbed a coffee from Carl's and something sweet to munch on later. Then I went to the hospital. I got to my daughter's room without bumping into anyone which I was happy about. This time it wouldn't be the sludge that was spilt but something much tastier.

I placed my cup and my coat on the table in the corner. Pecking my daughter on the forehead. I apologised for not being here last night not that she would have noticed either way.

Then I parked my butt down on the chair and picked up the book I had left here the day before. There was only twenty pages left but I didn't even get a chance to read one before Doctor Williams poked his head through the door. "Hey. The nurse told me you actually went home last night."

"I did but the chair is still comfier."

"There must be something wrong with your bed then." I might have gotten on with this doctor but that didn't mean I had to share personal details about my sleeping arrangements. "I wanted to ask you something last night but then I chickened out."

"Yes?" I placed the book back on the table expecting a question about my daughter.

"Would you like to go for dinner one night? Perhaps tonight?"

"What?" I couldn't believe he had just asked me out. There was an age gap between us but more so because I just didn't find myself sexy. He had seen me at my worse, asleep with dribble on my chin.

"I shouldn't have asked. Sorry to disturb you." The doctor turned and let the door shut behind him.

For a moment I was frozen to the seat. Unable to believe what had just happened. Then Kelly's words hit my mind. Telling me to jump up and rush to the door. "Doctor, wait."

He turned, smiling with his eyes more than his lips. "Call me Greg."

"Greg. I would love to grab some dinner. Tonight is fine."

He pulled a nice big smile and it creased the edges of his young eyes. "Great. I'll pick you up from here? Around half three. That way you can get back for the visiting hours."

"Perfect." We stood there staring at each other for a while before he turned and walked off. Never had I ever thought that I would get asked out by him. He was so young.

As I turned to return to my daughter I saw Doris sitting behind the nursing station. She too had a gigantic smile on her. "He's been building up the courage to do that for months now."

"Really?"

"Yep. And I'm glad he has because he kept asking me whether he should or not. It was becoming really annoying."

"Thank you."

"Don't mention it. Just make sure you have fun tonight."

"I'll try." As I returned to the room I found myself wondering what I should wear. The problem was, I didn't know what to expect. With how young he was maybe he would take me to grab a burger and chips. Or could he be taking me to a fancy restaurant. Outfits for both were extremely different.

I looked down at what I was wearing and decided it wouldn't make a good impression on a date. So I left the hospital after kissing my daughter and walked into town. I was happy to see the weather was better than yesterday.

Trying three clothes shops I finally found a nice flowery top that will go nicely with my jeans. As I arrived back at the hospital I walked through the entrance. Hitting into something solid. I had apologised automatically before even looking up at the pedestrian.

"We really have to stop running into each other, literally."

"Hey, Matt." I looked up into those eyes that seemed brighter than the day before. Then I saw what he was wearing. Yesterday it had been a nice suit. This time it was the opposite. Blue jeans with rips in them. A white t-shirt which clung to his every definition.

How could a man look so different just by a change of clothes?

Before he had been this wounded man I felt sorry for. Now I was finding it hard not to check out the way his short sleeves snugly hugged his biceps.

"Louise?"

"Yeah. Sorry. How are you doing today?"

"She passed away last night. Shortly after I got back."

"I'm so sorry for your loss."

"Unfortunately it happens. She won't be the last to lose their life in a mugging." His expression looked like it would crack into sadness at any slight touch. I was only used to that feeling in my own mind. No idea what to do when it was someone else. So I simply reached over and rubbed his upper arm, feeling the tense of muscle underneath.

"It'll be okay. It gets easier."

"I'm sure it will. So, it looks like this will be my last visit to the hospital. Unless I get hurt in the near future."

"Well I hope that doesn't happen."

"Thanks. But I wanted to give you my number and to say that I owe you dinner for running out on you yesterday. It is the least I can do since you managed to lift my spirits. I won't take no for an answer. And since my job is to stay home and write on a laptop, I'm free whenever you are. So call me when you want to grab a bite to eat."

"Um...." I wasn't too sure if he was asking me out on a date or if he was just being friendly. But two guys asking me out for food in the last hour was making me feel good. Better than I had even before my daughter's accident. "Sure. Sounds good."

"Great." He pulled a big smile which seemed out of place after hearing the bad news of his sister. But I couldn't help but get lost in how sexy it looked. It was like Kelly's comments about getting some had woken that part of me up. And the universe had decided to give me two guys at once. Who was I to say no to the universe?

I took his card from him. "I'll chat to you soon."

"I look forward to it." He leant down the nine inches difference and placed a soft kiss on my cheek. I was unable to stop myself from flushing red. In the past I had done a lot more than get a kiss on the cheek but it seemed the gap since the last time anyone showed me any form of affection hadn't gone unnoticed by my body.

So I sunk into that nervousness and turned as Matt walked off towards the entrance. My lips were curled in a big smile as I watched him move. Eyes dipping to those cheeks being hugged tight by the denim. It looked good and I found my fingertips itching to dig into those toned curves.

I was about to turn and make my way to my daughter's room when I noticed a blonde looking around. She looked familiar and a ringtone rang in my head. Her face had been on Greg's phone at the café. This woman looked even hotter in person. She saw Greg and her whole face lit up as she flicked strands of her blonde hair behind a shoulder.

I couldn't take seeing them together so I twisted on the spot and made my way to my daughter. Saying hello to Doris as I ducked into the room and took my usual perch in the chair. I wasn't in the mood to read. My mood was currently dragging me down.

All this time sitting here and watching my daughter not move or open her eyes. And yet this feeling seemed to trump that. Had I just gotten used to seeing her so still? Or was the new found affection turning my heart into a fragile crystal. A feeling I never cherished having.

I leant back on the cushion and let my eyes watch my daughter's face. The way she lied there, looking peaceful. And then I shut my eyes. Despite the amount of sleep I got last night I still managed to drift off. The soft beeping of the machine turned into ticking of a clock.

I looked up and saw that it was just after three o'clock. My date with Matt was soon. Jumping up from my seat I kissed my daughter and ran out of the room. I didn't like leaving so quickly, like I was running out on her but it seemed I was more excited about this date than I first thought.

Bursting out of the entrance to the hospital I looked around for Greg. Wanted to see those young eyes looking at me like I was the only woman in the world who could attract his stare.

Spinning until I lost my bearings I stopped and saw the white coat of a doctor. Looking up I saw the blonde hair that Greg had. Running over I grabbed his elbow and yanked him around.

But my eyes widened with horror as I saw his lips locked with a blonde woman. I could see their tongues dancing together. "Greg?"

He looked over and there were those eyes. Only they had lost that sparkle. Then I looked at the blonde he was kissing. It was the same woman that had been at the hospital before. The one who was on Matt's phone.

She pulled a wicked grin and then pulled the doctor back to her lips. Kissing him and pulling him to her body as she arched her back. Stepping away I found I couldn't look away. Eyes stuck on them as they breathed in each other as they kissed and moaned.

A hand touched my shoulder and I spun. Looking up at the tall man with that sexy grin. "Matt?"

"Louise. I'm glad I found you. I have something to tell you." But he didn't speak. His big arms wrapped me up and pulled me onto my tip-toes. That's when his lips touched mine and it felt like a firework had gone off inside my head. Scrambling every thought apart from the one that told me to let him take me.

To use those lips on me. I wanted to feel them touch and tease my skin. Every inch of it needed his attention and my skin seemed to hum at the idea. My fingers moved into his hair, stroking through the black strands. Sinking into the kiss like I had melted onto him.

A flash of bright light and I felt more than his lips against me. His skin felt so hot pressing to mine. Like it would leave a burn. Only I wasn't afraid of it. In fact, I wanted that heat to mark me as his and only his.

Another flash of light and that's exactly what I felt. But not only on my skin but inside me. A burn deep that heated me up. Boiled my brain of any logical thought. Then a third flash came and a loud beep rung out in my ears.

Eyes shot open and there was Doris standing in front me with a worried look on her face. I caught my breath and heavily regained the air in my lungs. Blinking to try and get rid of the image of Matt. Locking onto her face and forcing a smile. "Is everything okay?"

"I was going to ask you that? I haven't seen you tossing and turning in your sleep since the first few months."

"Um...." I felt a bead of sweat trickle down my temple. Rubbing it away and smiling again. "I'm okay. Just a dream, that's all."

"As long as you're sure you're okay."

"Yes. I'm fine. You should get back to your job. I'm fine, I promise." I waited until she left and then continued to suck air into my lungs. There was no way to explain why that dream had come to me. There had never been a dream so hot in a very, very long time. It had me gasping for breath and it had only felt like seconds.

I rubbed the back of my hand over my forehead and regained my composure. I checked my watch and saw it was just gone three. I continued to watch the seconds ticking by as I thought about my dream.

I didn't know who that blonde woman was but clearly I didn't like her. Otherwise she wouldn't have took Greg from me. Then Matt came along, saving me. Taking me so suddenly.

My memory brought back that feeling of him deep inside me. Right now I could still feel him there. His inches filling me perfectly and in such a way that my breathing started getting heavy again.

Swallowing helped a little but that thought was still there. Shaking my head I decided to get up and get moving back to the apartment. I need a shower after such a hot dream and quite possibly a very cold one.

So I stood up and made my goodbyes to my daughter. The warmth of her skin against my lips reminding me she wasn't gone. And then I left. Grabbing the next bus back for that cold shower.

As I stood there with the water moving with the curves of my body my mind went back to that dream. Not the painful part at the start but the end. The flashes of skin on skin. My heart beat matching the way it had felt.

My tongue slid to lick my bottom lip as my fingertips brushed my neck. Moving lower like it was being controlled by him. Like the thought of Matt and myself was moving my hand.

I felt the bump of my nipple on that curve. Tingling chills ran down my spine as I rubbed my palm across it. Breath gasped through my open lips. My hormones demanded more. Feeling my fingers touch across my naval.

I took a deep breath and pushed my hand down. Then a loud thudding came from the door. "Oi, Louise. I need to get in the shower to. I've got a hot date."

"Just finishing up." I quickly checked my hair for conditioner before turning the water off. Wrapping a big towel around myself I opened the door. Kelly was already in her underwear and her fingers were working on the bra clasp. "In a rush?"

"Yeah." She tried to push past me but I moved in her way. "Really, Louise?"

"Which student are you meeting up with tonight?"

"It's not a student tonight. I'm seeing my parents."

"Oh." I quickly moved to the side to let her jump into the room. Grabbing the pile of my clothes I shut the door and let her get ready. I could understand her nervousness since her parents hated that she became a teacher instead of going into the family business.

If they were meeting up for dinner then there must be something big coming up. I felt sorry for Kelly because that usually meant they were going to try and push her out of her career. But I knew Kelly was strong enough to keep her life here. It's what she had always wanted.

Once dressed again I stood in front of Kelly's full-length mirror. My faded blue jeans and that nice flowery top. The shoulders were cut out with flowing sleeves. I tied my hair back into a ponytail, leaving a few strands to dangle down either side of my face. Applying just enough makeup to make it look natural before heading for the door. Grabbing a handbag this time to carry my stuff in.

I shouted a good luck to Kelly as I left and headed down for the closest bus stop. As I travelled I couldn't keep my mind off of that dream. Feeling far too turned on than I should before a date.

Greg was standing out the front and I was happy to see he was alone. Even happier to see he was wearing something casual like me. And when I walked up he seemed very happy to see me. With his white teeth shining between his lips he opened his arms and pulled me in for a hug. My hormones skipped around as I felt that young body against mine. His muscles twitched and tensed as he held me.

When he did let go I looked up at his frowning expression. "I have no idea why I just did that." A nervous chuckle made me smile.

"I don't either but it was nice all the same."

"Good. Shall we walk?"

"It's not raining so why not." I automatically hooked my arm through his and we walked. We didn't talk much because I was simply enjoying the presence of a man. Being on a date with one. I hadn't realised until now that I had missed it so much. Getting lost in this feeling, I tip-toed up when he opened the door and pecked his smooth cheek.

Just a peck but I felt the warmth from him. And that smile he pulled had my hormones sitting up and taking notice. "After you, Miss Barnes."

"Oh please. Call me, Louise."

He smiled again. "With pleasure." I went through first and looked around. Having walked by this place many times over the years but never having stepped foot inside. It was famous for the chicken dishes which I was looking forward to finally tasting. The place wasn't busy since it was early.

A waiter came up and gave us one of those welcoming smiles. "Table for two?"

"Yes. Somewhere by the window, please." I gave Greg a look. He simply smiled down at me. "Thank you."

The waiter took us over to our table and gave us our menus. "If you come up to the counter when you're ready to order." He placed a little number by the condiments before walking off to welcome another couple who had come in.

I flipped open the colourful menu and started looking through the categories. It wasn't long before I found my meal and the sides that would go perfectly with it. I peered over the top of my menu and saw Greg just sitting there with his hands folded on the table. His menu still where the waiter had left it. "Not eating?"

"I've been here plenty of times. I know what I'm having already."

"Bring all your dates here, huh?"

"The last few times I've come here was with my younger brother. He loves the burgers they do here."

Smiling as he shared the first personal information about his life with me. "How old is he?"

"Twelve."

This had my mind ticking things over. I didn't want to ask this question but my mouth seemed to have a mind of its own. "So how old are you exactly?"

Greg smiled, "Worried I'm too young for you?"

"That depends on your answer."

He laughed but I didn't. In truth I was a little worried about it. "I'm twenty-five. Not that much younger am I?"

"Not a big gap, no."

"A gap you could get used to?"

"Maybe."

"I guess I'll just have to make sure I'm extra charming."

This time we both laughed and I found myself liking this doctor even more. "You can start by buying dinner."

"You honestly thought I was going to allow you to pay? Let's head up to the counter if you're ready."

"Oh I'm ready and starving." We both got up and went over to the cash register where we were greeted by another worker with a fake smile. They must train that kind of thing when they first get the job.

"Which table are you seated at?"

I went to look but Greg was already speaking before I could focus on the number. "Table four. And I will be having a chicken burger and can I double that up, please."

"Of course. What kind of spices would you like?"

"Hot, please. And could I get the tomato removed."

"Certainly. Sides?"

"Can I just get a big portion of fries?"

"Anything else?"

"Yes, please." I smiled at her as I looked back down at the menu to remind myself of what I wanted. "I'll have the chicken wrap. Mango and lime spices. And can I get the creamy potatoes and the garlic bread."

"Sure. Any drinks?"

Greg asked for two glasses for the soft drinks machine. The order was finished and Greg paid for the meal with a big smile. "First sign of charm."

I nudged my shoulder into his ribs. "Don't get too ahead of yourself." We got given an order number and I got given one of the empty glasses. I poured crushed ice into it from the machine and then chose the fizzy orange option.

Whilst Greg picked up some cutlery and napkins I made my way back to the table. Looking out the window as couples and friends walked by. My date plopped down in front of me with a straw. I took it from him and stuck it into my drink. He watched me with a soft smile as I took a sip. "What are you looking at?"

"Beauty."

I coughed as the liquid almost went down my wind pipe. "Laying it on a bit thick now aren't you?"

"Sorry. Coming on too strong?"

I laughed, "Possibly." I smiled at him. "I tend to find it hard to take compliments. More so when they suddenly come out of nowhere like that."

"So, do I need to send over a note to warn you of incoming compliments?"

"Cheeky can be a good sign. But you may also get a cheeky kick to your shin." Smiling and letting my tongue come out to point at him.

"Looks like I best watch myself then." He slipped a pen from his pocket and wrote something on one of the napkins.

He slid it over to me and I read it. *Incoming compliment.* My eyes shot up to him and I saw his mouth moving. But before he could say anything I kicked him in the shin possibly a little too hard.

Luckily Greg laughed as he rubbed it. "You have a mean kick."

"You have no idea, Doctor Williams."

"Here's to finding out more about each other then." As he rose his glass I clinked mine to his. And like we were signalling our waiter, that's when he brought over our food. I had to admit it was the best looking food I'd seen on date. The problem with that was, this was the first date I'd been on for over a decade. Back when I first met my daughter's father. One night is all it took for a family to be started.

He left shortly after the accident. Saying things were too tough and there were younger, easier women to please out there. So with this new take on my life now involving dating I dug into my food.

And it tasted just as good as it looked and I let out a moan of enjoyment. I caught Greg looking at me. I opened my mouth to talk but a piece of lettuce came tumbling out and embarrassment hit me hard.

He just chuckled lightly. "Maybe you should swallow before talking."

I finished chewing and swallowed the food. "Well I was taken by surprise when I caught you staring at me. See something you like?"

"Well I do love the food here." I flicked that piece of lettuce at him but it missed and hit the window. Leaving a lovely wet patch. "Amongst other things."

"Uh huh." I looked into his eyes and I saw the heat. My own desire matched his. I had no idea where this sudden truck load of lust had come from but it was hard to ignore it. Like floodgates being opened and I was going to embrace it.

My tongue slipped out and licked my lips. I watched his eyes dip to that movement. Greg smiled and I watched his own tongue do the same. My body moved forwards just as a voice came beside me. I looked up and saw the waiter standing there. "How is your food?"

"Um.... It's great. Thank you." The waiter smiled and walked away. As I turned back to Greg I saw the desire still there but the moment had gone. So I picked up some garlic bread and munched away.

After our main course and a lot of talking we ordered a dessert to share. It was a cinnamon waffle with three scoops of vanilla ice cream and the whole plate was drizzled with chocolate sauce.

When it arrived I was tempted to steal the whole thing. But I shared and I enjoyed every mouthful. Not to mention the looks I was getting from Greg. There were no words needed to describe what he was feeling. It was written all over his young face.

So we finished the delicious food and left with a voucher for our next visit. We walked around the city for a little bit. Getting to know each other but the whole time I was wondering how much more time it would be before he mentions his place.

We came to a fountain just outside one of the nicest hotels in the city. He sat on the concrete edge and tugged me down next to him. As his arm came around me I snuggled into him, enjoying his closeness.

Then I looked up at the view. The night had changed the way the place looked. Lights in windows and street lamps illuminated it in such a romantic way. Eyes meeting Greg's as he looked down at me. I stretched my body up, my lips touching his.

It started out as a simple kiss but when his hand hooked behind my neck it deepened quickly. I slid my body closer and my hand found his thigh. My fingers tightened around it as I got more turned on.

Those lips massaged mine and I slipped my tongue between his. It was soon met with the wet touch of his. Making me moan in response. I could feel his fingers slowly stroking through my hair.

I placed my hand against his chest and pushed closer. Pushed harder against him but he wasn't expecting it. I felt him move backwards but a little too far. When I opened my eyes I couldn't stop us from falling into the water with a loud splash.

Surfacing with a loud gasp I rubbed the water from my eyes and looked over at the drenched man.

Then a burst of laughter came from us both as we got weird looks from the people walking by.

Greg stood and pulled me up. But he didn't take me out of the water. He pulled me in and we were kissing again. I could feel people's eyes on us and the whispered comments but I didn't care. I didn't even care that my clothes were beyond wet and clinging to my body. I just wanted to feel those lips for a few more seconds.

But someone shouting broke us apart. I looked over the little cherub at the centre of the fountain and saw the doorman for the hotel running down the steps of the building. Waving his hand above his head and shouting at us to get out. Warning us he would call the police.

Suddenly I was being lifted up into the air and carried over to solid ground. He hopped over the side and grabbed my hand and we were running. We didn't stop until the hotel was a tiny block of bricks in the distance.

We turned a corner and placed our backs to the wall. It pressed my clothes to my skin making me shiver. "I think we need to get out of these clothes." I looked up at him, liking the way he was talking. "My place isn't too far if you don't mind the walk."

"I'm sure you can warm me up once we get back there."

His smile said it all and he grabbed my hand and we ran the whole way back. By the time we climbed the flights of stairs to his apartment I was out of breath. I leant back against the wall as he unlocked the door.

We walked through quickly. I didn't notice anything about his place. Turning around I got a second wind as soon as the door was shut. I leapt forwards, my hands grabbing handfuls of hair as we kissed.

His arms encircled me and pulled me tight to him. I pushed him back to the door and pressed myself on him. Letting him feel my breasts crushed into his chest. Our tongues tangled with each other's.

A gasp brushed over his lips as his hands found my arse roughly, lifting me off the ground. I couldn't help but wrap my legs around him. Needing to feel him as close as possible. I felt those fingers digging into my cheeks. My breathing becoming heavier as everything he did had me wanting more. My hormones were dancing around like it was a party.

I felt him carrying me but I couldn't say where. I was too busy lost in his touch. The way he carried me. I let my hands slip out of his hair and over those arms. Feeling the definition of his muscles. Such a strong man in control.

I was suddenly dropped. His bed cushioning my fall. I stared up at him with a huge smile. Eyes on him as he stood there. The grin he returned was devilish. And then he stripped. Any attempt I made to help him he pushed me back down.

So I lied there and watched with a big smile. Watching his fingers undo the buttons on his shirt. It slipped down his arms and I saw the bumps of his abs. The way his pecks flexed as he moved. I dug my teeth into my bottom lip as I kept watching.

I could feel myself getting wetter. The tingling between my thighs making my breath quicken. His hands moved down to his trousers. The belt came off and then he revealed his underwear. Tight, black and I could see that growing bulge. Knowing how I was effecting him.

As he stood there I slipped closer to the edge, unable to stop myself from touching him. To my delight he didn't stop me this time. So I stood and let a single fingertip run over his chest. The hardness of his muscles felt amazing as I trailed my touch lower. Moving over the bumps of his abs. Each time my fingertip dipped between them my body pulsed for him.

I tucked the tip into the waist band of his boxers, seeing the increase in that bulge. So I drew it from left to right, the end of my nail scratching lightly over his skin. I could see his chest rising and falling faster.

I removed my finger from his underwear and grabbed his wrists. Directing us, turning us and letting him sit back on the bed. Then I began a strip for him. Slipping my top off over my head. Letting my hands run over my breasts. Locking eyes with him as I did. Loving the way he looked at my body as I stripped further.

Dropping my jeans to the floor and stepping out of them. I moved a little closer as I arched my back, pushing my breasts out towards him. Arms reaching back and unclasping the material that covered them.

The bra slid down my arms and to a hooked finger. Tossing it to the side I let his eyes move over my curves. Feeling my nipples aching to be touched. My whole body starting to feel like that. Knowing my knickers were wet not just from the fountain. He could no doubt smell it in the air.

I hooked my thumbs into them and let them slowly fall down my legs. Standing completely naked, vulnerable to him. And god it felt so freeing. My eyes dropped to his bulge that was now a pole tenting in his underwear. I was even happier to see just how big a pole he had.

"Take those off." A smirk emerged at my order. It even surprised me at how in control I was with the situation. Expecting to be putty in his hands when we got back here. I could feel that restraint wavering as he slipped those boxers off. Finally getting my eyes on his thickness. It was so hard it just pointed up like it was standing to attention for inspection.

And I didn't want to disappoint it. Moving forwards slowly. Watching his eyes still moving over my exposed skin. One knee was placed to his left. The other to the right. Perched on the edge of the mattress with him beneath me. So hard and ready for me.

His hands slipped up my thighs and gripped my hips. Tugging me down I let him direct me. I drew in a deep, sudden breath when I felt him nudging against my lips. Parting them. A touch I hadn't felt for so long sending a lightning bolt through my thoughts.

Greg kept pulling me lower as his mushroomed head slipped against me. The anticipation of feeling that hardness inside me was almost unbearable. My head tilted back, my eyes shut. Just feeling him there as he entered me further. Pushing into my pussy and stretching my tightness. My breathing catching as I slipped lower. Feeling his inches deeper and deeper until my lips touched the base of his shaft.

Pressing my palm to his chest I stopped myself there. Holding him inside me, filling me like I haven't felt in years. Getting used to the way he stretched me. Greg's eyes looked up at mine as I sat astride him. "You okay?"

I couldn't help but let out a long sigh. "Oh god, yes." With my hand on his chest I pushed him back. Shaking the bed as he fell. Now with both hands over his hard muscles I started to move. Rising up and down slowly. Moaning as I feel him sliding between my lips.

The hum of pleasure filling me slowly as I kept rocking. Looking down at the expression on his face. Smiling as he let out a long moan. "Enjoying our date?"

He tried to lift his head up but I rolled my hips down upon him making it flop back as he let out another moan. Each time he made a noise my pussy clenched around him. Getting wetter the more I moved. Feeling his thick shaft massaging against my silk walls.

And the more we fucked the faster I got. That feeling of pleasure inside me building. Riding Greg harder. Feeling his head slamming deep inside me. I couldn't believe I had put off this feeling for so long.

My hormones singing in celebration at the act we were committing together.

I leant down and kissed him, hungrily sucking on his bottom lip as I bounced. My breasts rubbing up and down his chest. Feeling my hard nipples drawing over his skin sending more chills down my spine.

Slamming my body down upon his erection. Wanting it deeper inside me. Needing to feel both my release and his. My teeth biting into his shoulder as his arms pulled me closer. Then I felt his movements. Pounding his whole length inside me in full, solid thrusts. So fast it felt like he was constantly buried deep.

I tightened myself around him. Hard on his shaft. Not wanting it to stop. My breathing erratic. Hot breath hitting his shoulder with every thrust. My pleasure building inside my core and emanating out to my feet, curling my toes. Moaning louder and louder.

Everything slipping away from my mind as all I could feel and think about is the pleasure. Even the closeness of his body simply moulding into my own. Feeling at one with him as his thrusts became more urgent.

Then that unmistakable feeling of himself exploding inside me. Feeling that hot spunk hitting my walls, painting them with his cum. I hadn't felt that in a long time and I couldn't stop myself from falling into my orgasm.

My moans getting caught in my throat as my whole body rippled with pleasure. Teeth digging harder into Greg's shoulder as it rocked my body. My pussy clenching and cumming around his magnificent cock. Waves of juices covering him. Riding those delicious shakes.

Until I lost feeling in my limbs and I slumped on top of him. I moaned as the last few thrusts rocked me. Then he stopped, slowly sliding himself out of me. Feeling that absent warmth gone now. Just the trickle of our cum mixed together, leaking from me as I just laid there.

I couldn't move. Wiggling my toes to try and get the feeling back as Greg just hugged me and kissed my cheek. His lips brushing my ear as he whispered, "Well, that was an amazing end to a great date."

I tried to speak but it just came out as hot air. Then I tried again, "Yeah." Only managing the one word as I rolled my body onto the softness of his mattress. The great contrast from his hard body bringing me back to the world around me.

I shut my eyes and just let the final shivers of my orgasm leave my body. Unable to move a single finger. It had been a long time since anyone had given me an orgasm let alone one that had me feeling so satisfied.

My breathing finally became steady. Looking to my left I saw Greg watching me. "What?" My word came out as nothing more than a sigh.

"Just looking at something beautiful."

I let my hand move closer, running over his chest. Just feeling the hardness of his muscles had my mind thinking again. Though he seemed pretty spent at the moment. But he was young. I wondered how long his recovery rate would be.

I snuggled closer, curling my leg over his, rubbing my hot skin against his. Making sure my breasts pressed against his ribs. "Are you trying to start me up again?"

"Hmm, maybe. Do you think you'd be up for round two so quickly?"

"Why make you wait." His body moved with speed and aggression. Rolling on top of me. My arms pinned to the bed. I wrapped my legs around his waist, slowly getting tighter. Pulling him closer.

He pressed himself down to me and I was shocked how hard he was. "Surprised?"

I couldn't help but grin up at him right before he filled me again. A loud moan burst from my lips and we started fucking hot and passionate. All night long. Hours and hours of it until we were both too exhausted to even move to kiss. And that's how I fell asleep in his bed. Naked and completely satisfied. Exhausted because it had been so long since anything like this had happened.

Chapter 3

I awoke to the smell of food and coffee. When I opened my eyes I looked around the room. All I saw was furniture. I took a long sniff of the air and smelt the sausages and the bacon on the frying pan.

Climbing out of the bed my legs felt a little shaky. So instead of moving around the room for my clothing. I just wrapped Greg's sheet around my body. Making sure I showed enough of my leg as I moved out into the rest of the apartment.

My eyes slid over the large television and the nice black sofa that sat before it. Book shelves sat either side of the big screen. Spotting a few titles that I recognised but most were medical journals or text books.

Turning I leant against the doorway as I watched Greg frying up some meat in the kitchen. "That looks good."

Greg smiled over his shoulder. "The food or something else?"

I didn't reply, just simply pulled a grin and winked at him. "How long till it is ready because I'm starving after last night."

The sexy man wearing just his underwear

turned with the pan, dishing out the sausages and bacon onto two plates. "Here you go. I'm glad to see you need refuelling. Surprised I could walk again after last night."

"It was very hot." Grabbing a fork as he dropped some toast onto my plate. A sausage was poked and I started munching. The hot food filling that emptiness inside my stomach slowly. "And satisfying."

He carried over two glasses of orange juice and offered me one. I took it with a smile and sipped at the cool liquid. Soothing the burn inside my tummy from the hot food. Greg perched himself on his own chair at the table. Giving me a quick smile before he started his breakfast. "Are you working today?"

"Yeah. Should be out of the library by two. I'll be up at the hospital after that if you just happened to stop by."

"I'll make sure I do." He leant over the table and kissed me, holding my chin against his curled finger. Then we sat and finished our breakfast like a perfect couple. There were looks of desire thanks to the state of undress we were in.

Until he finished his meal. "I should get ready for work." As he came walking around I stuck my leg out from underneath the sheet. My skin on display as his eyes moved down over it. "Or I could stay for a little bit longer."

His hands came out and grabbed the sheet, tugging me up onto my feet. And there I stood as I pulled the sheet from my body. I felt the soft material slide down my skin sending a chill up and down my spine.

"How late do you want to be?"

Greg pulled a killer smile and I couldn't stop the smirk that hit my lips. "We'll just have to see how long we last."

His body came towards me but I placed my palm against his chest, feeling the hairless skin. "Hold on big boy." Standing there naked I let my eyes slowly move down over his muscles. Seeing the bulge growing in his underwear.

"We need to get rid of these." Lowering myself down to my knees. Licking my lips at the thought of not only seeing his cock again but tasting it this time. Feeling those tingles rising again between my thighs.

Curling my fingers I tugged down that material. Looking up into his eyes as his thickness sprung free of its confines. So close to my lips already I found myself licking them. Holding back for a moment as I kept my eyes locked on his.

My hand slowly wrapping around his shaft, feeling it throb inside my grip making me moan. The memories of how this thick erection stretched me last night. My hand moving, rubbing along those inches. Watching as his eyes closed, Greg tilting his head back against the wall. A moan slipping from his lips. Knowing how good it feels for him as a louder moan came rolling up his throat.

So I quickened my strokes, looking down to see his manhood oozing pre-cum. Rubbing my thumb over that little slit as my hand slipped up. Making his body shake with another moan. Then I stuck out my tongue. Slowly moving closer to him for that first taste. My mouth salivating at the thought.

My concentration breaking with a yelp when the apartment was filled with a shrill ringtone. I stopped as the doctor looked down at his phone on the counter. "Shit!"

"What's up?" Asking whilst my hand still stroked him. "You don't have to go in do you?"

"Hold on." He picked up his phone and answered it. "Doctor Williams." He made a few grunts for the phone and some moaning from my movements. "Okay, I'll be there in ten minutes."

The phone was hung up and he looked down with frustration in his eyes. "Problem?" Asking even though I already knew the answer.

"Unfortunately, yes. I have to go in, now. No being late for me I'm afraid."

"That is unfortunate." Still stroking him from tip to base. "So you have to leave right now?"

"You know, you are one hot tease."

I bit my bottom lip as I thought about licking his cock. Just to have a taste. "I always thought that was a good thing."

"It is but I do have to go and believe me when I say I wish I didn't. I could spend all day with you, never leaving this apartment."

"That sounds great for a second date." I let my hand slip from him. My palm feeling so empty. Pushing myself to my feet. Looking down at his arousal with an arched eyebrow. "It is a shame."

The doctor let out a moan of annoyance. "Tell

me about it." Greg leaned in and pecked my lips softly before running off to his room to get dressed. I sat and finished my meal, not bothering to cover up again. Greg came rushing out gathering his things as he spoke to me. "Feel free to stay as long as you like. The door will lock automatically behind you. And I'll see you at the hospital later."

He grinned as he came over for a kiss. "Until I see you again." Flashing back my own smile before he disappeared. Making a bacon sandwich with what was left on my plate before finding my clothes. The whole time I couldn't stop my smile. Or my thoughts of last night.

Practically skipping around the place, getting dressed piece by piece. Not even bothered by the dampness. Taking an apple from the fridge before leaving his building. On my way home I didn't rush. Simply dawdled across the city happily, humming to a tune that popped into my head.

It was almost midday by the time I had gotten dressed into something dry and got to the hospital. So I grabbed something small from the hospital shop with some sludge and walked up to my daughter's room. Doris was sitting at the nurse's station when I arrived. She noticed the massive smile still on my face. "What's gotten you in such a good mood?"

She asked but I could tell by the look she was giving me she knew exactly what had happened. So I simply just shrugged and smiled. Backing into the door I entered into my daughter's space.

Turning I saw her lying there quiet as a mouse.

Like always except this time that horrible knotted ball in my stomach didn't hurt so much. It was still there and never would go away. But last night and what had happened between me and the hot doctor, made it easier to cope with. Which I never thought would ever happen.

So I sat down and grabbed one of my books from the table on my right. The day went by as I munched on my apple and read the book. I had gotten through a few chapters when a familiar head came poking through the door.

"Hello, doctor."

"Miss Barnes. How are you doing today?" I saw his eyes shift to the nurse just outside the door.

"Don't worry. Doris already knows."

I knew he didn't really care because of the smile he pulled. "Oh." He allowed the door to shut and walked over to me. As he leant down I saw his lips purse ready to kiss my cheek but he stopped inches away.

I noticed his head look over towards my daughter. "What's wrong?"

"Should I be doing this in front of your daughter?"

"Shut up and kiss me." My fingers gripped his shirt and pulled his lips down to mine. A hard kiss sending shivers through my body. Reminding of the way we kissed last night and all the other fun we had. Letting my tongue tease against his bottom lip before pushing him away. "See, nothing bad happened."

"No. Something very good did though." He

pecked my lips before standing up and clearing his throat. I sat there quietly as he did his usual checks but my mind was busy. Watching his body moving and thinking about how it looked under those clothes.

Thinking about all the things I would want to do with him. Or to him. When he was over with those checks he did something he never had done before. I watched as he slowly moved over to me and sat down on the other chair that had never been used since my daughter had moved into this room.

Greg leant forwards and placed his elbows onto his knees. "So how are you doing?"

"I'm doing fine. You?"

"A little frustrated we couldn't finish our breakfast together." His eyebrows did a little dance.

"Maybe another time." My bottom lip curled into my mouth and I bit it slowly. He watched the movement. "Just so you know, I don't usually do something like that. Jumping into bed on the first date. It had been a long time and you are extremely handsome."

"Why thank you. I didn't think that so don't worry." He pulled that clean-cut smile of handsomeness at me. "So are we going out again? Tonight?"

"You ready for round two so quick after the first?"

"I was ready this morning." That hint of fire in his eyes flamed for a flicker. "But I can wait."

Honestly I was thinking about throwing him down on the floor right now but that wasn't me. I couldn't give in to my hormones around this man every time. We'd always be naked. Or at least naked enough to have sex.

"Tonight works for me. What time shall we say?"

"How about you come around my apartment for six. I'll do you some dinner. Then...."

"I'll do you for dessert." I cut him off with a wink.

The doctor laughed, "That sounds better than my roast pork."

"I do love a good roast."

"In that case we should enjoy both parts of the night." I couldn't resist biting my lip again. Like it was starting to become an involuntary thing when it came to Greg and his good looks.

"I shall look forward to my tea then."

"I'll look forward to my dessert." He leant forwards and kissed my mouth. Letting me taste him as his tongue danced with mine. Sending those hormones skipping around.

"Tease." The doctor stood without replying and walked out the door. Flashing me a quick grin over his shoulder before it shut. As I leant back I let out a long sigh like I was trying to relieve the pressure of horniness from inside my body.

So to try and distract myself I picked up my book and pushed through the pages. Reading and trying to lose my head inside the story. It was hard but I managed to right before my stomach started grumbling for food.

Looking at the watch it wasn't time for my home cooked meal yet but my stomach was kicking up a storm. So I went down to the cafeteria just to grab something small. Something that wouldn't spoil my appetite for food.

It ended up being a blueberry muffin. The treat was wildly over-priced but my stomach wouldn't let me forget I needed it. Still grumbling as I walked back to my daughter's room.

Munching on the muffin and reading the time passed until it was close enough for me to head home. So that's what I did. Hopping on and off the bus. As I opened the door I was attacked with a tight hug.

Kelly's hug squeezed the air out of my lungs. "Easy. I can't breathe."

"Oh, sorry." She let go and gave me a cheeky grin. "You need to tell me everything."

"What do you mean?"

"I know you didn't come home last night. At all. And that smile tells me that you didn't sleep at the hospital. You look like you've slept in a bed but there wasn't much sleeping involved. Come on you need to tell me everything."

She stood there, blocking my way into the rest of the apartment. "Fine but only if you get out of my way. I need to get ready."

"Wait, you're going out again? Two nights in a row? Lucky guy."

"Lucky me." Sticking my tongue out at her I moved into the apartment. Grabbing a change of clothes and a set of underwear from my suitcase. The clothing was a lot more casual but still looked good on me. The underwear however was one of my few lingerie sets I owned. I always loved how black lace looked against my skin.

Shutting the bathroom door I shouted through the wood to Kelly standing on the other side. "We went out for dinner and then went back to his."

"I figured that much out myself. Tell me everything."

"Nosey."

"Yeah, just spill. How good was it?"

I couldn't believe how red my cheeks went at her question. "It was fantastic." A shriek came through the door. "Calm down."

"Oh come on. You finally got laid. It's been ages."

"Far too long."

"Precisely. So he's a doctor and he's great in bed. What more could you ask for?"

"We're just taking it casual at the moment. Nothing too serious. I don't think." I looked at the mirror and realised I was saying it more to myself then to her. There was no need to rush into something serious especially after one date. But she was right. He was a doctor and he could give me such amazing orgasms. They were two, very big ticks in the pro column.

"Casual means lots of sex."

"Coming from you?"

"I'm an expert." Kelly laughed. "So what's on the cards for tonight?"

"He's cooking dinner for me and I'm giving him dessert."

"I bet you are." Smiling at her remark, I got dressed and looked at myself in the mirror. Applying some lipstick and pulling my hair back into a loose ponytail. I looked good and I felt good. The perfect combination for a hot night in.

I opened the door almost dropping Kelly to the floor. "Do you want me to call after we have sex to fill you in on all the details?"

"After? Hell, call me during." She grinned.

"Naughty." I pushed past her and went onto the tiles of the kitchen to grab a glass of orange juice. Kelly followed me like a dog following a bone. "How did the meal go with your parents?"

"Next question."

Eyes flicking to hers as I took a sip of my juice. "Fair enough. What do you have planned for tonight?"

"Tutoring a promising young man."

"Tutoring him in what?" I arched my eyebrow at her.

"Something he will use for many years to come."

"Sounds like he'll get a great education."

"I'm lucky as well in this case. He's a very quick learner."

"You should open up a school." She looked off into the distance like she was actually considering it. "I was kidding. God. Imagine the teacher/parent meetings at that place." We both laughed out loud. "You'd have to hire some more staff. For the female students."

"Sorry, guys only. So you wouldn't be able to enrol."

"I don't need lessons."

"I'll ask the doctor about that."

"Don't you dare." I grabbed a tea bag from the little pot and chucked it at her. I missed but she didn't manage to catch it either. "Lucky you won't be doing sports at the school."

"That was a terrible throw."

I didn't reply but just walked out after emptying the glass into my stomach. "Be gentle with the poor guy."

"Being gentle isn't an option with this one. He's built like a house."

"Judging by your grin he's built big in other departments as well."

"You know me, I don't kiss and tell." I pulled a shocked face. "Okay, just go. He'll be here soon."

"Have fun." Pulling the door open I went to move out into the hallway but a large body blocked my way. I looked up at the smile. If it wasn't for his large size I would have called him cute. "You must be my friend's student."

"Um.. yeah." He looked past me and saw Kelly. His eyes pulsed with passion.

"Come in. And be good you two." Winking at Kelly before leaving the building and getting off at my stop. My phone rung just as I started walking.

The cold air wrapped around me as I answered without looking at the screen, tugging my arms around me. "Hello?"

"Hey, it is Greg. I have some bad news."

"Oh no."

"I'm going to have to cancel tonight. Been trying to get out of the hospital for an hour now. And I've just been told the on call doctor has called out sick. I'm the next on the list so it is my job now."

"I could still pop round though couldn't I? If you're just on call."

I heard the smile in his voice. "That's really sweet. But I stay at the hospital when on call, not at home."

"Oh. Okay. We'll just have to have dinner and dessert another time."

"Sounds great. I will text or call you in the morning."

"Sure. I look forward to it." He made a kissing noise before hanging up. And I stood there on the spot. I was all dressed up and I had nowhere to go. There was no point heading back to the apartment because Kelly was there with her student. Teaching him god knows what.

I thought about heading to the hospital. But I caught my reflection in a shop window. All dressed up, why waste this at the hospital. Looking down at my phone I saw Matt's name in my contacts. So I called up the writer who answered with a sleepy voice, "Hello?"

"Matt, it's Louise."

His voice suddenly sounded more alert. "Hey, you. How are you doing?"

"I'm good. My plans actually fell through and

I'm all dressed but no one to spend tonight with." I knew how that sounded when it came out but I couldn't change it now. "Would you like to grab that dinner?"

"Yeah. Would be my pleasure. I'll be in the centre in ten minutes. I assume you're there."

"I am. I can see a restaurant called The Garden."

"I've been there before. Fantastic food. Bit pricey."

"Good thing you're paying then."

His chuckle floated out of the phone and kissed my ear. "Good point. I'll see you there."

"Sure." As I put my phone back into my pocket I headed over to the restaurant. I moved through the green double doors and the soft, rhythmic music came to my ears. Like stepping out of England and into Spain.

The gorgeous woman with her impossibly long blonde hair smiled as I entered. "How may we help you?"

"I'm just waiting for someone. Is it okay if I sit inside?" I pointed to the sofas to my left that sat against the front window.

"Of course it is. Let me bring you a coffee to warm you up." Without an answer from me she walked off towards a door labelled, kitchen. When she came back she was carrying a big black tray. It matched her black outfit which clung to that stick thin body.

She placed it down. Sitting atop it was an upside down mug. Milk, sugar and a pot of coffee.

"Enjoy."

"Thank you." I was surprised there wasn't a price involved. It was like she did this off her own back. The woman returned to her post behind that little podium and waited for someone to enter.

I sat and drank and just enjoyed the ambience of the restaurant. The steaming liquid heating my body temperature up nicely. Only six minutes had passed when the door opened again. I heard the woman's greeting.

When I looked up I saw Matt standing there looking down at me. He was wearing a black suit which fit him too well. His white shirt unbuttoned at the neck. Cufflinks shined under the lights.

I had read somewhere that a suit was like lingerie for men and they had been right in this case. Matt looked good. I stood and walked over to him. "Hi. Nice suit."

"You look very nice tonight as well. Thank you for giving me a call. It was going to be a microwave cooked meal tonight." I found it funny that someone with enough money to dine here in a suit like that would be eating a microwave meal. "Shall we?"

"Yes." He offered me his arm and I curled my fingers around it.

"Table for two please."

"Right away, sir." The woman grabbed our menus and led us across the place. Most of the tables were already taken by couples and families. All of who were better dressed than I was, including the children.

The hostess took us to a table secured in a little

alcove giving us some privacy from the others. Matt let me sit on the booth section against the wall. He took the one opposite with his back to the room. The lady gave him and then me a menu. As I grabbed it I commented, "Thank you for the coffee."

"It was my pleasure. A waiter will be by soon to take your drinks. Have a perfect meal." A huge smile was shone down upon us before she walked away.

Opening the menu, the first thing I noticed were the prices. Realising how they could afford to give away coffee for people waiting. This place was extortionate. Peering over the menu I looked at Matt. He smiled back when he caught my eyes, "Everything okay?"

"Are you sure you can afford these prices?"

"I'm sure. Don't worry about the money."

"I feel bad though."

"This is my treat for you being so nice. So, don't worry about the price and get whatever you want."

A waiter came walking over with his long hair pulled back into a neat bun. "Can I get you two some drinks?"

"Yes." Matt took charge of the situation. "We shall have the special red. The bottle, please."

"Right away, Sir."

"Thank you." The man walked off and I stared at Matt with disbelief. "I hope red is okay."

"Yeah. I'm just not used to a guy taking charge like that." Watching his reaction. Getting a big smile in return. A soft sigh slipping through my lips. "Red will be great."

"Good. Have you had a chance to look at the food?"

"Not yet."

"Well." He placed his menu down on the table which I copied. "The fish here is superb. Like they've nipped out fishing and brought back the catch fresh. Then there is the pasta. Italian chefs couldn't make a better one. Of course you have the roast. They do a different one each night. All the trimmings of course."

My gut had been craving roast ever since Greg had mentioned it. "Oh I'm definitely having the roast. I was supposed to have it tonight."

"Two roasts it is then." Matt grinned at me and the waiter brought over our bottle of wine like he had heard we were ready to order the food. The bottle was put down on the edge of the table with two glasses. Matt grabbed it before the waiter had a chance to. "Allow me. And we shall have two of your roasts. Please."

"Right away, sir." The waiter smiled and left us alone to enjoy each other's company. Matt slowly filled my wine glass up and then his. Lifting my drink to my nose and sniffing. The scent of fruit wafting up my nostrils. Smelling so sweet I couldn't resist a sip. My tongue bathing in the taste of the wine. Never had anything that was this good. A soft moan showed how much I enjoyed it.

"It is a very nice wine isn't it?"

"Yes." I took another sip before placing it back down on the wood. Licking my lips. "Have you been here before?"

"Once or twice."

"It is a very nice place."

"Wait until you try the food. You'll think you've died and gone to heaven."

"I can't wait." I leant forwards on my elbows and studied his face. There was slight stubble which I usually didn't find attractive. And whilst this wasn't a date I couldn't help but look at him like it was.

His eyes lifting to mine and he froze. "What? Have I got something on my face?"

"No. Just looking."

Matt grinned and sat back. "How's your daughter?"

"Nothing has changed."

"Stupid question, wasn't it."

"Yeah but people can't help but ask it."

"Human nature I suppose."

"You should know about human nature. Being a writer and all."

"You'd think that wouldn't you. But I find I'm more surprised by people now than I ever was."

I sipped the wine as he spoke. "So what did you do before hand? If you don't mind me asking."

"Of course I don't. Feel free to ask anything." Watching as he raised his glass to those lips. The way he pursed them so gently to take a drink. My lips parting just a touch as my mind fuzzed for a moment. "I worked at a firm."

"A lawyer?" Licking my lips as I blinked and brought myself back to the conversation.

"No, nothing like that. We would get hired

by businesses to help them with negotiations and bringing things in their favour through take overs and such things. Boring work really."

"How did you manage to go from that to writing?"

"Actually, it was my ex-wife's idea."

"Your ex-wife?" My voice was full of surprise but I wasn't entirely sure why.

"Yeah. She always said I had a good eye for a story. She kept pushing me into it. I used the money I got to allow me time to knuckle down. Give it my all. Then an agent, publishers. The rest is history, really."

"Well I'm glad you got out of the job you didn't like."

"Thanks. I'm much happier now." The waiter walked over with our roasts. When the food was placed before me I couldn't believe the size of it. Four thick slices of today's roast which just happened to be my favourite, chicken.

With those slices of meat were potatoes, stuffing, carrots and a few pigs in blankets. It wasn't the usual size of a meal you would get at a posh restaurant. It was massive and I didn't think I'd be able to finish it all myself. I saw the look of hunger in Matt's eyes when he looked at his meal.

Feeling my stomach grumbling at the fact I hadn't started eating yet. "Looks good."

"Yes it does. Enough food for you?"

"Might be too much." I giggled as I picked up my knife and fork. "I'll see how I get on." And we both dug into the food. Every piece of it was delicious.

Each bite made me silently moan in my head. My taste buds being treated like they were royalty. We made comments to each other whilst we ate but there was no getting in between us and the food.

So it was only when most of it had gone and I was starting to feel full when I made the first proper sentence in a while. "That was absolutely amazing. You can officially scratch the debt clear. It has been paid in full and then some."

"Really is a perfect place for a meal isn't it. And it has been my pleasure. Great food and great company."

"Thanks." I smiled as red filled my cheeks. "Are you planning on getting dessert?"

"They actually don't do dessert here."

"Really? I think this is the first place I've been to that doesn't."

"Well they used to. But they found people didn't order any because the main meals were too filling. So they just kept the size of their meals and took away the desserts. So no ice cream for you I'm afraid."

"It's okay. I hadn't planned on having a dessert tonight any way." My memory went back to last night's treat. And what I was supposed to have tonight. Remembering the feel of Greg's body against mine and the way he filled that most intimate part of me.

The waiter walked over to us with a big smile. "Are you two finished?"

"Yes we are." Matt smiled at me as the waiter

picked up our plates.

The man's eyes went to the leftover food. "Do you need a doggy bag?"

Giving him a sweet smile. "No, thank you. But everything was perfect. Thank you so much."

"Thank you for coming to our restaurant tonight. I'll pass your comments onto the chefs after I've brought your bill over."

"Thank you again." Matt dug around in his suit jacket and pulled out a wallet. Then a shiny silver card. The man with the ponytail came back with the slip of paper and two mints. He spotted the card in Matt's hand. "I'll be back with the card machine."

As he walked off my hand moved towards the bill but Matt was quicker. "I'm paying. I don't want you knowing how much."

"Why not?" I tried to grab it out of his hand but he pulled it out of reach just in time.

"Because I saw your face when you saw the prices. You don't need to know how much the meals were. Okay?"

"Fine." I narrowed my eyes at him but honestly I was fine with it. That was the idea behind tonight, repaying me. So I was happy to sit there and let him. I grabbed one of the mints and bit into it. Looking at the small bits of biscuit, the minty scent filling my nose.

Finishing it off as we stood and walked out after Matt paid. The blonde by the door gave us a big smile and told us to have a great night. "That place has just jumped to the top list of the best restaurants I've ever been to."

Matt laughed lightly. "Did you drive here?"

"Tonight's over is it?"

His smile turning to one filled with cheekiness. "What did you have in mind?"

"Don't get any ideas, Mister." He laughed. "How about we walk around for a little. Get to know each other more." Matt turned and offered his arm to me for the second time tonight. "Such a gentleman."

"At first." He sent me a wink before we set off. We crossed over the road and started walking the perimeter around the big park in the city. At this time of night there wasn't much going on. A few night time events happening but nothing too exciting.

"So how's the third book coming along?"

"Well. I have some research set up for tomorrow night."

Lifting my eyebrows as I gave him a quick look. "Anything fun?"

I could see the look he gave me out the corner of his eye. "Any research when it comes to writing an erotica book is fun." There was a short pause before he added. "Maybe you should come along. See what you think of my work."

"Tempting." It really was tempting and the curious part of me wanted to say yes. "I'll have to pass on that." Thinking about dropping the subject but my curiosity was in a playful mood tonight, "But, what kind of research would it be?"

"Curious about it aren't you?"

"Maybe a little."

I looked and saw the devilish grin he was

pulling. "If you did come with me you would need to wear a nice dress. Wouldn't need any money or anything. Just come with a smile and enjoy."

"Enjoy what?" My fingers gripping onto his arm tighter. My need to know was growing and he was clearly playing with me.

"That would be telling, wouldn't it." Matt winked at me and then started talking about the scenery around us like it was no big deal.

"No, no. Don't change the subject. You can't tell me something like that and not divulge more."

"Well, you'll just have to come along to find out, won't you." That grin came again and I couldn't stop my lips from curling in reply.

Taking a deep breath as I looked away. Hoping the cool air would calm my body. "Dream on, writer boy." I leant my head against his shoulder as we walked around the park. The wind whistled through the branches. The walk was both peaceful and fun. "So how are you doing after your sister's passing?"

"Oh." The sudden change in topic seemed to have caught him off guard. Feeling his arm slipping from mine. "I'm doing okay, I guess."

"Sorry. I shouldn't have asked. We were having a really nice night and now I've ruined it." I felt awful and I found myself looking down at my feet as we walked.

I felt his finger tug up my chin to look at him. "It's okay. Was just a surprise. That's all. You haven't ruined anything because I'm still enjoying your company."

"I'm enjoying yours as well."

"So what were you going to be up to when you called me? Sounded like an afterthought kind of thing."

My mind wondered whether I should tell him or not. Whilst this wasn't a date I still felt a little bad about it. But I blew out a sigh and smiled. "I was supposed to have a date."

"Oh wow. And there was me thinking I was the only handsome man in your life."

"Think of yourself as handsome do you?"

"I do own a mirror, you know." Usually that kind of arrogance would be off putting but somehow Matt managed to make it work and it went so well with that killer smile he kept throwing at me. If I hadn't had amazing sex last night, I think my hormones would have persuaded me to jump him right here. A good way to describe him would be, sex on legs.

"How modest of you."

"Why thank you. Don't think I hadn't noticed how hot you're looking tonight."

A chuckle escaped my lips. "I'm not exactly dressed to impress."

"And yet you still look beautiful." Matt suddenly stopped and turned me towards him. As I stood, looking up, I watched as his eyes slowly made their way down my body. Usually that would have made me squirm. I always got embarrassed in this kind of situation but somehow his stare was burning hot.

"What are you looking at?" I involuntarily stuck out my chest as his eyes came back up. Arching my back so my top clung to those curves in my bra.

"I could say a thousand things about you. All compliments but I feel you're the kind of person who shrugs off compliments for something small and meaningless because you don't feel you deserve them. So I will just say that you, standing before me right now, make me smile."

I was expecting something rude. Something I would find in one of his books. However when he did speak, my breath caught in my throat with surprise. "I suppose that is one compliment I can see is true." Looking up at that smile and the way his lips seemed to glisten under the street lamps.

I lifted myself onto my tip-toes and kissed them. Nothing amazing, just a simple peck and to my delight Matt didn't try and make it something it wasn't. He simply smiled again and didn't even ask what it was for. Like his male mind could comprehend that I was saying thank you for his words. Maybe he was pretty good at reading female nature thanks to his research.

I was offered his arm once again and we carried on walking. Chatting and getting to know one another. The second man in my life couldn't be more unlike the first. He walked me to the closest bus stop and left me there with a tight hug.

When I got home I walked into the apartment and called out, "Kelly?" I didn't get an answer and as I walked further into the apartment I noticed the mess.

A lamp was lying on the floor and there was broken glass on the tiles of the kitchen.

I picked it up and called out her name again with no answer. Once it was all cleared up and placed in the sink I ventured into her room. The covers were messy and clothes were on the floor. Nothing out of the ordinary after a night with one of her students.

So I turned back around and went to sit on the sofa. It wasn't long before my phone rang in my pocket. When I saw it was Greg's number I smiled uncontrollably. Hitting the answer button. "Hey, you."

There was a long pause before he spoke. "It's nice to hear your voice but I have some bad news. Your room-mate, Kelly, is in the hospital with a cracked rib and a lot of bruising."

"What?!"

"She was brought in a couple of minutes ago. A neighbour called the ambulance. You should get down here."

"Yeah. I'll be there as soon as I can."

"I'll be here when you do."

"Thanks." I hung up on the doctor and rushed back out the door. The apartment locking behind me. Grabbing a taxi instead of the bus to cut down travel time. Rushing through the door with my stomach knotted in terror. Moving through the corridors I got to accident and emergency.

I saw the blonde hair of my man and pushed through the curtain. He spun around as I rushed over to the bed and looked at Kelly. I could barely recognise her with the way her face had swelled up. One eye closed shut. The bruising was already showing.

Greg's hand touched my shoulder. I turned full of anger at the sight of my friend like this. "What happened?"

"Pieces are being put together by the police. Your neighbour is in the cafeteria giving her statement. They'll be up to check on Kelly to see if she is able to make a statement."

I looked over at her. She was asleep at the moment and even if she could talk would they be able to understand her with this much damage. "I don't think she'll be able to help just yet."

"They might want to speak with you now that you're here."

"Okay. I'll be right here if they need me." I took the seat beside her and instinctively looked over to the table. Only there wasn't my usual lump of books there. I thought about my daughter lying in her bed in the other department.

But I settled in because Kelly needed me more at the moment. And Greg had been right about the police. Ten minutes later and a head popped through the curtain. Her partner stood outside like he was on guard.

I stood from my chair. "Hi. My name is Louise. I live with Kelly."

"Where were you last night?"

"Out with a friend. I wish I hadn't left. Do you know what happened?"

"Your neighbour told us she heard shouting and a lot of banging at around nine-thirty. Things went silent and someone left the apartment in a hurry. She knocked but there was no answer. She went back into her apartment but after hearing nothing for a half hour she went inside and found your roommate in her bedroom, beaten to a pulp."

"So it was the guy who she was with tonight?"

"There's no way to be sure but it's likely. Do you know his name or what he looks like?"

"I don't know the name but I got a good look at him when I left."

"Do you think you could come down to the station and talk to one of our sketch artists? Put a face to this guy."

"Sure. I do know that he is one of her students. She teaches at the university."

"She was seeing one of her students?"

"Yeah." I knew I had gotten her into trouble for that. Maybe not with the police but if the university found out then she would get fired. Then again, the police investigation would have uncovered that any way.

"Thank you for your time. Please, come down to the station as soon as possible."

"I'll be down there in a little bit."

"Great. Thank you, miss?"

"Barnes."

"Thank you, Miss Barnes." I got a smile and the officer grabbed her partner on her way out. I gave Kelly's forehead a soft peck before saying goodbye. There wasn't much response in her but I'm sure she heard it all the same.

I grabbed Greg on the way out and gave him a kiss to the cheek. "Hell of a night."

"Yeah. Sorry about being on call."

"Don't be. If you had been with me, I might not have found out about Kelly. So, thank you."

"My pleasure. I'll have to make sure I do the roast for another night."

"I'll hold you to that." I gave his other cheek a peck before leaving the large building. Walking up the road and around a few corners until the precinct came into view. Sitting for what seemed like forever, describing every detail I could remember. The final sketch was spot on. Even staring at the student in pencil form made me angry.

By the time I got back home I was in no mood to get undressed. Simply laying down in my clothes and drifting off to sleep. Dreaming deeply about the writer in my life. And it wasn't a soft dream either. It was hot and passionate.

Chapter 4

When I did wake up in the morning my clothes were drenched with sweat. It hadn't been hot last night so I could only blame the dream I had. Even now I found my breathing a little heavier than usual.

Revitalising my body with a shower and setting off to work. Once I was there I sat at my usual spot and found myself thinking about Matt. That dream last night had felt real enough to trick my mind in feeling his touch even now as I sat in the library.

My mind thinking about his offer to help him with research. I couldn't even think of what he could be getting up to. But my curiosity was peaked. Not to mention the thought of seeing Matt again made me smile.

I grabbed my phone and sent him a text simply asking how he was and if the invitation to research tonight was still open. Then I waited for what seemed like forever. Helping customers until there was a soft beep from below the counter.

I opened it up and my smile half disappeared. Even though his research was put back a night he was willing to take me out for a drink. He asked me what place I wanted to go to. Instead of having a conversation over texts I took my break and called him from outside the building.

Matt answered like he had his phone already in his hand. "Hey, Louise."

"Hey. I figured you would know a place to drink. Since you've had more of a single life than I have."

"I may know about a place or two. I'll let it be a surprise then."

"What should I wear?"

"Something similar to last night. Casual but sexy."

I smiled at his compliment telling myself to take it. "Thanks. Where should I meet you?"

"Send me your address and I'll come pick you up."

"Sounds great." So we hung up and I texted him my address.

As I hit the send button a male voice came to me. "Looks like I caught you on your break."

I looked up and saw Greg strolling over to me holding two coffee cups from the café a few buildings down. "Hey. What are you doing here?"

"Figured I'd come surprise you since you said you were working today."

"That's really sweet of you. You didn't have to bring me a coffee."

"And a croissant. Apparently they were made fresh this morning but I didn't know if I should believe the teenager behind the counter or not."

He gave me the coffee and passed over the little

bag. "You not eating anything?"

"After a shift like last night, I think I'll wait. How's yours?"

"It's okay. Nothing exciting happens at the library so pretty uneventful. Nothing like being a doctor."

"I'm sure it has its moments." He tugged me down to the bench that sits just outside the entrance. "At least it pays the bills."

"Yeah. How is Kelly doing?"

"She's awake. There's no lasting damage. The police came back and took her statement and they're looking for the guy."

"I hope they catch him and lock him up for what he did."

Greg put his arm around me and pulled me close. "I'm sure they will."

"Thanks for the coffee. And the food."

"You don't have to thank me." I opened the little bag and started munching on the croissant. We ended up sharing it. Chatting quietly until my break was over. Before he left Greg pulled me to him softly and kissed my lips. His tongue breaking between them, massaging mine.

I moaned into his mouth as it deepened and I let my tongue respond in kind. My whole body seemed to hum with the need to have him. Flashes from the other night. Pushing my body to his, wanting to feel it skin on skin.

The kiss slowed and he backed away. "That and more to come on our next date. I promise."

"Looks like the list of things you owe me is growing." I thought about mentioning Matt. About tea last night and drinks tonight. But I didn't want him getting the wrong idea, to think I was dating two guys at once. Even though there was nothing wrong with that. I didn't want to upset the sweet man. No point whacking a bee hive with a stick when there was no need to.

"I'll let you know when I'm free again. Looks like I have another night on call ahead of me."

"Well, give me a call when you get a break. Be nice to hear your voice." Greg gave me a flash of his white teeth before walking off. I returned to work and thanks to his visit the remaining hours went by like a flash.

It felt weird going back to an empty apartment especially since I technically didn't live there. But I wasn't there for long. I stripped, grabbed a quick shower, then got dressed in something a little sexier than what I wore last night.

Tight fitting, black jeans. Wanting to show off my best feature, giving it a quick look over my shoulder in the mirror. A navy top with the back showing strips of skin from left to right. A strapless bra and lacy knickers that matched the colour. I checked my outfit in the reflection.

This might not be a date but wanting to look good had nothing to do with that. When I looked good, I felt good in my own skin. That in turn helped me be more confident. Taking a deep breath, feeling butterflies in my stomach.

With time to spare I decided to use Kelly's curler to give my hair a nice bounce. The buzzer for the front door filled the apartment as I was nearly done. So I quickly finished curling the last strand and I answered the call. "Matt?"

"Yeah. You ready? Taxi is waiting."

"Almost, just have to do my makeup."

"That's not almost ready. Let me up, we can grab another taxi."

"Alright." I hit the button on the intercom and left the door ajar so I could go back to getting ready. Then I turned and saw the state of the place. Kelly wasn't the tidiest of people to live with.

So the next minute I spent rushing around trying to clear things up. Shoving dirty dishes in the sink and flinging my clothes back behind the sofa where they wouldn't be seen. Carrying two wine glasses from the coffee table in front of the television I heard Matt's voice. "You apply makeup with wine glasses? No wonder you girls take so long."

Looking up, giving him an eye-roll. "Very funny."

"I thought so." He walked over to me and took the glasses out of my hands. "Sink?"

"Please."

Giving him the once over, seeing that he was in his more casual clothing. A pair of dark jeans with a nice white shirt. Heading back into the bedroom to do my makeup. Applying the eyeliner when his voice came through the doorway. "And where should I put these?"

Standing up I moved to see what he was going on about. Spotting him standing there with a g-string hanging from a finger. "Oh my god." I rushed over and snatched it from his finger and threw it behind the sofa where the rest of my stuff was hiding. "Do you always go snooping through people's underwear?"

"Do you always keep your underwear on the coffee table?" I didn't remember seeing them there and I saw the cheeky look he was giving me. "Anyway, I'm just a little upset you're not wearing those tonight."

I looked over my shoulder as I walked back over to my makeup. "How do you know I'm not wearing something sexier?"

"Oh, I'm sure you are." He grinned and started to follow me.

Putting up my hand and wagging my finger at him. "This is a no-Matt area. Just in case you're thinking of anything naughty."

"I would never." Laughing as he pulled an over the top shocked face. That quickly vanished when he saw all the products I had laid out on Kelly's dresser. "What you wearing tonight then?"

"Something lacy." I gave him a wink.

Words slipping through his laughter. "No, I mean makeup wise."

"Oh."

"But thanks for the mental image." His eyes dropped to my arse as I was bent a little at the waist. My cheeks blushed as I pushed it out with a little sway. Seeing his eyes come back to hold my stare. "So?"

"I was thinking of going with a purple look."

"That would look nice. Try those, with those."
His hands moved in the air, pointing out products.
Matching colours that would work well together. I
looked up at him as he was finished. "Like I said, I
do research. It's bloody hard writing from a woman's
perspective."

"I can see why. We're not exactly the most
easiest to understand."

"But you are fun. Women in general, I mean."

"I know what you mean." I took his selection
of makeup and started applying it. Getting helpful
tips from him which was really weird. Once finished
I turned to him, letting him study my work. "Well?
How do I look?" Matt smiled and then leant down,
pressing is lips to mine. A gentle, single kiss before he
stood upright. "That good huh?"

"Yes but that's the easiest way to smooth out
lipstick."

"Any excuse to give me a kiss."

"Why do you think I picked the super stay
lipstick?"

Biting my lip so he wouldn't see the massive
grin that was about to appear. "You are very cheeky."

"Whenever I can. It's part of my charm."

"Who said you were charming?" Giving my face
a final look in the mirror. The purple was subtle, a
quick take and you wouldn't realise I was wearing
any apart from the eye shadow. Happy with it I stood
upright.

"You look beautiful but that has nothing to do

with the makeup."

Looking over to him I could see the sincerity in his look. He may flirt with me and his looks weren't subtle at all. But I saw a different side to him when he spoke like that. "Now that you are all done up, we've got a reservation to keep."

"Reservation? I thought we were going for a drink."

"We are but there are so many different ways to enjoy a drink in this fine city. I'm going to show you one way. Then maybe another if you're interested."

"This wouldn't have anything to do with research for your book, would it?" Arching an eyebrow at him.

"Don't look at me like that. Yes, this place gave me the idea for the first book in this trilogy. However, there is no sex or anything rude involved. So you have nothing to worry about."

"Okay. I may regret thinking this way but I trust you."

"To a certain extent hopefully. You're far too smart to trust me fully."

Laughing, "I think you're pretty harmless." I grabbed my small bag from behind the sofa and we left. Walking out into the wind we started on foot. Waving hands at taxis as they whizzed past. Most of the walk I spent it snuggled up against his body. Trying to steal his warmth thanks to the large, thick coat he wore.

The next time he stuck a hand out and whistled the taxi slowly pulled over to the side of the road. We managed to get inside just as the rain started spitting down. The droplets pinging atop the metal roof. Matt gave the address to the driver.

I stared out the window as the buildings gave way to countryside and then back to even larger buildings as we switched from residential to the business area of the city. The yellow car pulled over to the side. Matt paid and we climbed out.

The music from the place we were drinking was soft at the moment. The line at the entrance carried on going off and around the corner. My eyes rose to the neon sign over the double doors. To me it was just a squiggle of blue and green light. Couldn't even make out letters let alone what the place was called.

My fingers gripped Matt's coat as we started walking up to the bouncer who stood in our way. "What is this place called?"

"Marie's."

"That says Marie's?"

"I think it was just a pattern she liked."

"You know her well?"

"We've go some history. Probably the cleanest way I could describe it."

I laughed. "Do I need to worry about you tonight? Leaving me for a barmaid or two?"

He looked down at me with his hazel eyes. "Tonight it is you and only you that holds my attention."

"Thanks." Matt got a kiss on the cheek for his sweetness.

"Any excuse to give me a kiss, huh?"

"Have to make sure the lipstick works after all." Giving his cheek a wipe with my finger.

The bouncer shifted sideways as we got to the steps. "Back of the line, please."

"I'm a member." Matt dug out his wallet and flipped out a golden card with the same pattern as the sign etched into the metal. "A golden member."

"Sorry, sir. Please head in and have a great night."

"Thank you." We passed by the lump in the suit. Matt checked his coat in with the petite girl in the cloakroom. As he came back my eyes slowly shifted over that shirt. Seeing his arms tensing under the material as he rolled up his sleeves. "You shouldn't stare. It's rude."

"Shut it." Giggling as we walked down the short hallway to the main room. The bar was lit up on the right with chairs and tables dotted around the floor. To our left was a line of booths that were semi-private.

Further over was a massive stage which stuck out a few metres towards the tables. Thick red curtains were draped down from the ceiling. Big bulbs of different colours lined the front curve. It was lit up by three large spotlights but no one was up there at the moment.

Matt stopped us at a little podium and a host came over when she spotted us. She looked good in her black dress. Her hair was so dark and perfectly cut it looked like a wig. Matching the way the rest of the waitresses wore theirs.

"I have a reservation under Carla Saint."

"Right over here, sir."

As we walked over I nudged him with my elbow. "Carla Saint? Pretty name."

"It's the name I write under. A male name can close many doors in the erotica world."

"But why did you book the reservation under that name?"

"Because the owner, Marie, is a big fan. She helped me with the first book."

"Whilst helping with your need for sex?"

"Envious?" He smiled and nudged me back as we were taken to the booth nearest the stage. We were seated and the host pointed to the menus at the back of the table. Then she left us there to our own devices.

I leant across the red leather and nipped one of the cocktail menus from the stand. Looking at the names of the drinks I started getting a little suspicious of this place. "I thought you said this wasn't a rude kind of place?"

"What do you mean?"

"All these cocktails are named after sex positions."

He leant over the table between us and had a look. "Oh yeah. Well I wasn't telling a lie. This place isn't like that. They're just drinks. These ones are a lot more normal." Matt plucked another menu and swapped them.

I looked at the names on this one and saw that they were the usual you'd find in any bar. "I don't know, I think doggy style sounded fun."

"With the right partner." I giggled at his wink before a loud voice came over the speakers around the room.

"Ladies and gentlemen, please welcome to the stage the first half of tonight's entertainment. The Calendar Girls." I looked up to the stage as the woman with the microphone walked off. Her wig-perfect hair swinging as she came down the steps.

Then the lights went down, small red lamps sitting on the tables illuminated the area. Footsteps tapped over the stage and the curtain was pulled up. Three spotlights hit the bodies up there.

Four women stood posed, wearing very short skirts and bikini tops. I gave Matt a look which he shrugged to. When I turned back the music start thumping out of the speakers and they began dancing. I enjoyed it as they moved to the music.

I hadn't even noticed Matt leaving the table until he came back with two cocktails. Bright green with a little umbrella sticking out of it. "Thank you."

"Thought I'd get you a doggy style."

"A man after my own heart." Winking as I took a sip. Getting a huge hit of fruit and a hint of a strong alcohol afterwards. My eyes shifting back to the stage as I sucked on my straw. Catching the chicks just as they whipped off their skirts, flinging them into the audience. Showing their bikini bottoms which didn't cover up much. "I can see why you like coming here."

"Look around. How many women do you see here?"

I pulled a face at him but I did what he asked.

Watching the crowd I did see more women than I thought I would and they were all cheering and enjoying the show just as much as the guys. "What gives?"

"Just wait and see." The song slowly came to an end and the women stood there, breathing heavily which made those bikini tops move up and down. The microphone wielding woman arrived back on stage.

"And the other half for you tonight. The Baker Boys."

I looked over at Matt who grinned at me before four hunky men came walking out onto the stage wearing denim dungarees. Their arms looked massive compared to the petite chicks standing with them.

All eight of them smiled as the music kicked back up again. The couples danced together in big groups and one on one. Halfway through the men were stripped of their blue denim and were revealed to only be wearing black G-strings. I laughed as they kept dancing. Gyrating together with the women.

It was most definitely something I had never expected to watch on stage but it was tasteful and I wasn't ashamed to say I was enjoying it. The dancers took a break after a couple of songs but were soon back on and dancing with more enthusiasm than before. Matt and myself were also running up quite a tab with cocktails. This was the most I'd drunk in a long time and I was feeling the effects of the alcohol.

Through the night I found Matt got more and more attractive. Noticing how my eyes lingered longer and longer. My thoughts moving from wanting to kiss his lips to wanting to rip his clothes off. It was all heightened by the fact that he was a gentleman. Sure he flirted but it was all harmless. It was the sweetness he projected that was pulling me towards him.

As the group kept entertaining the crowd Matt walked back up to the bar. Watching his jeans tightly cup his arse cheeks. My mind tussling with control, feeling the need for him. Shaking my head and looking at my empty glass. Whispering to myself, "It's just the drink. Calm down." Blowing out a few breaths.

Lifting my head as a body came to sit opposite me. A woman sat there with a smile. Tight black curls bouncing from that movement. She wasn't dressed like the other staff but she didn't look like a customer either. My eyes catching her nose stud shining under the lights. My eyebrows rising as I asked, "Can I help you?"

"I'm sorry for staring. But you're the most normal looking girl I've seen Matt bring here."

I looked over to my friend at the bar but it looked like I wasn't going to get any help soon with how busy the bartenders were. "How do you know Matt?"

"We first met when he was a lonely writer. I noticed the kind of stuff he was writing when I read his laptop screen in a coffee shop. We got talking and I told him to come here and watch a few shows. Matt, the cutie that he is, even put me in his book."

"Are you one of the main characters?" I looked over to the bar again but Matt still hadn't been served yet.

"No, no. I'm the lesbian bar owner where the female character works."

My attention was snapped back to her. I looked into her dark eyes as I swallowed over the lump in my throat. "Did you not mind being written as a lesbian?"

"It's my life choice. No need to be ashamed about it."

"So you're a lesbian?" Wishing that my drunk mind would catch up quicker.

"From the top of my head to the tips of my toes. How about you?" She leant forwards on her elbows. Feeling her bare foot brushing against my calf. "Ever thought of coming to the more fun side of the game?"

"Not since college."

"That's a shame. Maybe you just need a helping hand." Watching her hands sliding across the table slowly. Long black nails tapped against the surface as they got closer. Instinctively I pulled mine onto my lap which brought out a rich laugh from her lips so loud I could hear it over the music.

"What's so funny?"

"You. Your innocence is so out of place here. I admit, I find it very attractive. So be careful. I just might have a taste." She leant forwards and her pink tongue slipped out, rubbing over her black lipstick. I couldn't resist letting my eyes follow the trip it made. The way it glistened under the lights of the club. "Have you ever had the pleasure of a woman's knowledge down between your legs?"

"What?" My breath came out as a puff of air. I filled my lungs up quickly trying to regain my composure. "No I haven't."

"Would you like to? I own the place. There's a lovely private room I reserve for special guests. You fit under that criteria. And I would love to taste your sweetest essence." As she smiled I could see the twinkle of playfulness in her eyes.

There was something about that look that had me leaning forwards against the table. Marie's smile increased as I drew closer. "And what criteria would that be?" I felt myself being pulled further into conversation.

Marie matched my movement, bringing us closer. Our lips inches away. Feeling her hot breath hitting my mouth. Making me lick them unintentionally. Her voice laced with lust, "Delicious."

I told my body to move back. To move away from her but it refused. She had a hold on me that I couldn't shrug off. A deep voice to my side made me break eye contact. "I see you've met, Marie."

"Huh?" I understood that it was Matt and I heard his words but somehow my brain didn't comprehend them.

He nodded me over and slipped in beside me. "I said, you've met Marie."

"Um. Yeah. She's...." My eyes flicking to hers. "Certainly something."

Matt turned to her. "This one is off bounds."

Marie sat back and held her hands up. "Sorry. Had no idea she was yours."

"She's not but I don't think she's up for your corruptible spirit."

"I'll take that as a compliment."

"And so you should."

I watched the two of them sparring with their words. "How's the book coming along?"

"Good. I'll make sure you get a copy before everyone else."

"I look forward to reading what I get up this time." She slid to her feet like a predator and leant down to give Matt a peck to the cheek.

"It's never as naughty as what you really get up to."

"Never." I heard him grunt as she bit his earlobe before stalking off through her business.

My eyes following her. "She's a free spirit kind of girl."

Matt gave out another grunt. "That's one way to describe her. I could think of a few more."

"Well you are the writer." There was a pause as the dancers finished up and the music dropped to a slow song. "She's a lesbian."

"You catch on quick, Louise."

"But you said you two had sex."

"If you cast your mind back. You implied we had sex. I just didn't correct you. Figured she might pop over to see me at some point."

I took a sip from the cocktail he had slid in front of me. This one was black with a swirl of white floating around like smoke in the night. Tasting a strong hit of coffee with a chase of vodka.

My eyes looked past him and spotted Marie standing by one of the tables. Using her lethal charisma on another woman. Only this time the victim looked a lot more interested in her than I did.

The writer gently nudged me with his shoulder. "You don't want to go there."

"Huh?" I looked into his eyes. "What are you on about?"

"Marie. She will eat you alive."

"Funny, that's practically what she told me would happen."

Matt's face was a picture of shock and amazement. "Thinking about popping to the other side?"

"Want to hold my hand whilst I do?"

His face was a picture that made me giggle again. "I think this place is bringing out your naughty side a little too much."

"Who says it's the place." I nudged into him before sipping more of my drink. The coffee hit my taste buds again. That vodka lingering on my tongue as my eyes moved from Marie and to the man to my left. My mind losing its inhibitions thanks to the many cocktails.

Biting my lip when his eyes hit mine. A second that stretched on, my tongue coming out to lick my bottom lip. My mind flipped a coin. The silver catching the light of my imagination as it dropped and I smiled.

Shifting on the booth seat and swinging my leg over Matt's lap. Straddling him as I pressed my knees to the seat. Slowly lowering myself onto his crotch. The face he pulled had me fitting with giggles. "Something wrong?"

His touch curled around my thighs. Inching up until they gripped my hips lightly. "Why would anything be wrong?" His eyes finally lifting to mine. A grin that had me biting my lip. My mind swimming with thoughts that had me grinding down on him. Rolling my hips, creating that heated friction between us. Matt's eyes getting a little glazed over. "I just want to know, is this the alcohol or am I just one of the luckiest guys around?"

I tilted my head left and right. Pretending to think about his question as I kept my hips rolling. Making him wait as my weight pushed down. The increase in his blood flow was pressing up against me and that just made me feel even hotter. Knowing how much he wanted me. "Maybe a little of both." It started out that it would just be a tease. To play him at his flirting game. Only now that I was rubbing over that growing bulge. "Are you really going to miss this chance by over thinking it?"

Another roll of my hips brought out a groan from his throat. "You know I've never been an over-thinker. But what about this guy you've been dating? I don't want to be stepping on any toes and I mean, it's hardly fair on him."

"Very confident of yourself. And we've been on one date and had sex. Nothing is written in stone just yet."

"So if I did this?" He leant forward and all I felt was the wet tip of his tongue run along my bottom lip slowly. A shiver running down my spine as it teased from one corner of my mouth to the other.

Matt leant back against the booth and I stared into his eyes, feeling my lust for him growing like a storm. "I wouldn't get into trouble?"

I let out a long sigh to try and slow my heart beat. "You would only get into trouble if you do that again but don't follow it up with something else."

"Like?" He pulled a massive smile that was full of mischief.

"Like that tongue touching my other lips." I leant forward and my own tongue came out. Flicking against his mouth, parting those lips. Allowing my hot breath to puff against his mouth as I lingered there. My tongue poised just outside of his parted lips.

Holding until I felt his muscles tense and he moved forward. Snapping my head back out of reach and I giggled. "See, it's not nice being teased. Is it?"

"I don't know. Depends."

"On?" Giving my hips a deeper roll. Grinding up that length of bulging meat.

"Maybe it would be better to show you some time. But right now." Hands gripped me, holding me against his body as his lips came to my ear. Hearing his words in a whisper. "All I can think about is fucking you."

A gasp of a sigh came out of me. Grinning wide as I replied quietly. "Then what are you waiting for?"

"Come with me." His words a growl of need and want. Without a warning he stood up from the booth, holding me there in his arms with ease like I weighed nothing. I was plopped down onto my feet and dragged off through the room.

Moving this way and that, dodging tables and chairs until we came to an abrupt stop near the bar. I noticed Matt talking to Marie who kept giving me looks but all I could think about was the writer.

With Greg it was all mutual actions. This time I felt like a school girl heading behind the bike sheds for a first kiss. I watched him talking until he was passed a key card and the dragging started again.

I allowed him to lead me because I couldn't stop thinking about his hands. Thinking about the places they would touch. My breathing was ragged as we passed through a few doors and finally came to a private room.

The dark purple matched the darkening of my thoughts. A bar sat in the corner with a gorgeous sofa next to it. Only my eyes were fixated on the king-sized bed. Walking over to it my fingers brushed over the fitted sheet. Deep red silk would feel amazing against my skin. Almost as amazing as Matt would.

Turning to find him right in front of me. Our eyes meeting with a hold that had me breath catching. His closeness making my heart race. Breathing heavier, feeling my curves rising and falling. Brushing against his chest so softly.

His eyes seemed so dark as they stared down at me. His breath coming out in huffs. Letting my tongue slip out slowly. And there we held ourselves. Both of us refusing to make the first move.

Sinking deeper into our stare I almost missed that fluttery touch of his thumb. Sucking in a short gasp as it skimmed under the front of my top. Making a burning trail up my side.

My breathing became erratic as it moved over my skin. My top bunched over his forearm as he hiked it higher. Feeling it press to the underside of my bra. Closing my eyes as his touch kept moving. Circling around my body to the clasp. The pop came from a pinch and it loosened from my curves.

His hand appeared and I followed its movement out the corners of my eyes as my bra straps were slipped down my shoulders. The support lessening until a hooked finger pulled it out completely.

The underwear tossed away. My nipples stiffened against the material of my top. No doubt so obvious to Matt. Only his eyes never left mine to have a look. Our stare burning to an inferno as his finger touched my skin again.

Moving up my belly and between my breasts. It nudged up my cleavage. My eyes blinked as I felt his touch causing electric chills to run to my nipples. Making then ache to be touched. All I wanted to do was give in. To have my head fall back and a moan erupt from my lips. My body was begging me to give in to him but I was stubborn. I would not let go of the small amount of control I thought I had.

Which was even harder to accomplish as his thumb brushed over the swell of my breast. Moving in circles as it neared the centre. My back arched instinctively as it drew even closer. Holding my breath, my nipple pulsing with the anticipation.

Finally feeling it trip over my areola and I let

out my breath in a soft moan. I heard Matt snigger as his thumb slipped from my breast without touching that aching nub. Slipping across my skin, the heat of it burning. Feeling sweat forming at the top of my neck. His thumb circling again but faster. Feeling it nudge against my nipple and running over it firmly. Moaning again I quickly bit my lip to stop myself. Annoyed at how fantastic he was at torturing my body with just one digit.

My tongue came out and ran over my dry lips. His smile curling as his other hand pressed to my tummy. Pushing my hips forward as I felt his fingers slide down. The pop of my jeans being opened. Then the noise of my zip.

My breathing couldn't be classed as anything but ragged. Unable to keep anything under control as his palm pressed flat to my stomach. He pushed me back until I felt the wall behind me. Licking my lips again as his hand moved. A thumb dipping into my naval before I felt his fingertips slip into my lacy knickers.

They explored lower making me arch my whole body. Moving my lips close enough to brush over his. I felt his tongue slip out and I allowed my own to meet it. And then his lips crashed into mine. My hands gripping his shirt tightly, pulling him closer. My hips shoving forwards as our passion fuelled my actions. My mind full of a swirl of need and want.

All my senses going crazy. Letting out a yelp as my nipple was pinching and tugged. My breast jiggling free as a pleasure pulse shot through my brain. Weakening my resolve even though it was just a slither at this point.

Kissing him until his fingers touched down over my mound. Shifting my legs apart, needing more of that touch. Biting his bottom lip with a groan as his middle finger slipped between my petals. Hands running up into his hair, body stretching on tip-toes as his finger slid up and down.

"Oh, Matt." My words nothing more than whispered gasps. That finger curling and dipping deeper. It nudged against me, making me moan again. Shutting my eyes and focusing on that feeling. I spread around him as he pressed. Allowing him further inside my body.

My head pulled my lips from his. Leaning it against the wall with my mouth open, breathing out moan after moan as he fingered me. Moving my legs wider, hips rolling to burn that hotness. Our actions spurring the other to move faster. I didn't have the state of mind to open my eyes and look at him. Just enough to keep myself up on my feet, arms wrapped around his neck. The pleasure built inside my core. I dug my teeth into my lip to stop from screaming out.

Opening my eyes when I felt his finger slip free from me. The absence felt horrible, my need for him growing more wild. Opening my mouth to speak when two fingers stretched me open. A noise came out in a hurry, not a moan or a groan. Just a pure noise of pleasure.

And with each thrust of his fingers came another and another. Getting faster just like my breathing. It felt so good and I could feel myself getting so wet. Knowing I must be covering his hand with how much he was turning me on.

My body squirming between him and the wall. Feeling the sudden emptiness as he slid his fingers from me. Gritting my teeth and burning my stare into his. "Don't fucking stop." Grabbing him roughly and yanking him in for a kiss. Shoving my tongue into his mouth.

His finger sliding up my slit to the tip. Feeling it curl and press against that swollen button. Every muscle in my body tensed as he flicked his fingertip around in circles. Moaning against his lips my fingers grabbed handfuls of his hair, grabbed anything they could. My toes curling, feet stretching up. Feeling the muscles in my thighs quivering. My slick walls pulsing and clenching.

His fingertip felt like a battery. Shooting sparks deep in my core. Nothing but moans escaping my lips as the pleasure built quickly. It just kept going, Matt didn't let up or slow down. Constantly running his touch over that button. Up and down, round in circles. The more I moaned and enjoyed that gorgeous pleasure the more pressure he used.

The storm inside my body raging harder. Growing as he touched me so perfectly until I was screaming with every erratic breath. So loud I drowned everything else out as my body cracked and gave in to that waterfall of pleasure and I orgasmed.

Feeling my gush of juices rushing out of me as he kept moving that finger. Kept topping up that pleasure as I pressed against his touch. Screaming out as my body shook and quivered. Non-stop shots of hotness hitting my body. Dowsing my brain in ecstasy.

My whole body on fire until it got too much. Grabbing his wrist and pulling his touch from that over-sensitive clit. My breathing slowing as the pleasure slipped away, allowing some slither of consciousness to come back. Blinking my eyes as the after shocks of something so amazing ran through my body. Making me jolt and suck in a breath.

Leaning against the wall, my arm around his neck, holding me upright. Rolling my ankles, feeling my thighs shaking a little. Looking up at him as he drew his hand from my knickers. Seeing how much I had marked him with my juices.

Then he did something I had never witnessed. Matt slid his fingers into his mouth. Letting out a moan that seemed to call to my hormones. He was tasting me and god I found it so hot. My eyes locked on that action until he pulled them out clean.

Finding my breathing was still weak as I spoke. "That felt amazing."

"I'm glad you thought so. You felt amazing to touch. And taste." I looked down at the bulge in his trousers. The writer laughed. "As you can tell."

"You better get that out and fuck me with it." His hands spun me around so fast I gasped. Hands tugged at my jeans until my bottom was exposed to him. I looked over my shoulder.

"Don't move." I gave him a nod as he stepped back. Standing there with my hands against the wall.

My jeans and drenched knickers bunched around my thighs. The cool air all over my arse like it was his look that was touching me.

Watching as he unbuttoned his shirt. Showing off those muscles as they tensed and rippled with his movements. That shirt getting tossed to the floor. Grinning at how amazing he looked.

Then those jeans were taken off. So damn slow I wanted to help him but his words had me staying in my position. Eyes drinking in his tented underwear. The black material slowly being pulled down. His cock straining against it until it sprung free.

My mouth dropping open. Matt was the longest I had ever seen. But damn, his cock was so thick. That fat head dribbling with clear pre-cum. Loving how it pointed straight at me. Making me want him even more.

Arching my body. Sticking out my arse and wiggling it from side to side. Waving it at him until he took a step closer. Turning my head to look at the wall. Eyes closing, hearing his footsteps bringing him closer.

Allowing my skint to feel for him. My breath catching when I felt his hand touch to my hip. His fingers wrapping around with a light grip, holding me there as he came closer. Feeling that press between my thighs. Rubbing up and down, using my leaking cum to lube up that fat head.

Then he pushed softly, slowly. Feeling myself stretching over him. Taking in that head with a sudden pop. A moan coming from my lips. The pleasure was immense even compared to how good his fingers had felt. Pushing back, sliding further down that length. My lips tightly rubbing over his inches until I felt my arse cheeks touch his tummy.

So full of him, that feeling making my head go a little light. Rolling my hips which made him moan. Smiling at that noise as I did it again. Then his hands grabbed my hips to hold me still. Giving him a little look over my shoulder. Eyes open wide giving him my innocent look.

Then he moved. Sliding out then back in slowly. Holding me in place so I couldn't quicken those movements. So damn slow and it was such a delicious torture. Both enjoying it but also craving something harder.

So I reached back and dug my nails into his arse cheek. "I said fuck me."

With a grin he made my wish come true. My hips used to pull me back as he started to ram deep into me. My surprised yelp quickly gave way to the immense pleasure of feeling him penetrating me. That rigid cock massaging my wet walls. Clenching down on him, wanking him with my pussy.

I slide my hand up under my top to a bare breast. My nipple aching for attention I trap it between my thumb and forefinger. Every time he stretches and fills me I roll that nipple. Pinching it between my grip.

My body getting sent to heaven as my body starts to build up that pleasure. Racing towards that climax so damn fast it makes it hard to breathe.

Panting out as my body responds to his intense fucking. "I'm going to cum again, Matt. Please don't fucking stop."

"Cum and I'll cum with you." My breathing sent crazy at his words and my body responded to them. The pleasure leaking out over his erection as he kept ploughing into my wet sex.

"Fuck. Keep going. I'm clos....." My last word was taking over by my scream as my body was hit by another orgasm. Grinding back onto his thrusts. Wanting it deeper. Needing it deeper.

Matt grunted and groaned and I felt his wet release. Covering my walls as he kept fucking my clenching pussy. Both of us filling the room with noises of pleasure as we kept grinding together.

My fingernails scratching over his thigh. Body jolting with the force of that amazing pounding. The pleasure releasing hard in waves until they faded. Allowing me to float back down to reality. It wasn't until we were both still that he spoke in that breathless puff. "Wow."

Licking my lips and grinning wide. "Wow." Moaning as I felt him slip free from that mess. Rolling around to face him. I looked down, seeing our mixture of cum making his spent cock shine. "That was...." I couldn't finish my sentence as I let out a long breath.

"I know. Certainly didn't think that was going to happen tonight."

"You shouldn't try and predict what will happen with me."

"I've learnt my lesson. And what a hell of a

lesson to learn." Teeth flashed through his grin.

"I should hope so." My shaking legs managed to carry me to the long sofa. The soft velvet feeling nice against my skin as I slumped down. "I need to get the feeling back into my legs."

"That good, huh?"

"I sense you're the kind of man who doesn't need any more help growing an ego."

"Well if you know you're good I don't think you can class it as an ego."

"Such an egotistical thing to say." And such a thing would ordinarily put me off of a guy. Only this wasn't like that. This was just fun and he was the right man for the job to bring me such fun.

Eyes watching him walk over towards me. Happy to see a few unstable steps of his own. Eyes swiftly lifting up over those muscles. He looked like a model with a body like that. So much definition I found it hard to remember he was only a writer.

I leant my head against the back of the sofa and there we sat. Completely naked and chatting like we weren't. All the way up until closing time early in the morning. It was a fantastic night in all ways possible.

Chapter 5

After being dropped off at the empty apartment I showered to get all the sweat and the smell of sex from my pores and then fell asleep. I was exhausted and even chose Kelly's bed over the sofa.

When I awoke to my alarm I got dressed with a skip in my step and a smile on my lips. Work flew past. On my break I went and searched for Matt's first book of his trilogy. I could feel myself getting worked up as I sat there on the bench outside reading it. Imagining all those touches to be his.

Thanks to my visit last night I could imagine Marie's perfectly. Even her character was spot on. I found myself laughing out loud at some of the stuff she said which got me some strange looks from people walking by.

At the end of my shift I signed out the book and took it to the hospital. It was between lunch and tea when I got there so I grabbed the usual snacks from the hospital shop and made my way up to my daughter's room.

I poked my head in and saw her laying there. The soft beeping of the machines filling my ears. My ritual of kissing her forehead and sitting in my seat was seen through. Reading further into the book I had gotten today.

Matt was a terrific writer and I could tell that he must have had some fun with his research. Then I remembered his invite to join him for some tonight. My lips wouldn't stop until they curled into a big grin at the thought.

Just as my mind was about to go for a swim in the gutter the door slowly opened and Greg popped his head. "Hey. Bad time?"

"No. I was just reading. Come in." All of a sudden I felt a ball of guilt building up inside me. Last night I was so sure it wouldn't be against the rules but now seeing his boyish good looks it had me thinking the opposite.

"What you reading there?"

"Just something I picked up at the library." I placed the book in the far corner of the table face down. "How have you been?"

"So tired. But I wanted to give you this." He came through the door and produced a small white box. It looked so fancy and I saw the name of a dessert shop on the side. "Wasn't sure if you would be hungry but it looked so yummy sitting in the window."

I took it and opened the top allowing the sides to fall away and reveal the strawberry dessert. My eyes took in the layers. Short cake, strawberry mousse and a whole strawberry sitting on top. It was only small and would take just two bites to devour but it looked too good to eat. "It looks beautiful."

"It tastes delicious. Go on, try some."

I picked it up and cut it in half with my teeth. The tastes of it mixed on my tongue and sent my buds ablaze. The dessert tasted better than anything I'd had before. So I quickly chomped the other half and swallowed. "You were right." I stood and gave him a little peck to the lips.

When I pulled my head back I saw the cute smile and I felt even worse about last night. So instead of thinking logically and coming out with what happened to see what he thought. My hormones decided to take over and I pulled him down to my lips. My tongue quickly moving into his mouth to play with his.

I pushed him to the door and my hand cupped his manhood. But Greg didn't react the way I had wanted. His hands pushed mine away and he broke our kiss. He was smiling but I could see the confusion and anger in his eyes. "What are you doing?"

"I just thought since we couldn't the other night, that I'd reward you for my dessert."

"Here? I could lose my job. There will be time for all that. But I did promise you a meal before we got to all that. Just be patient." Greg's lips touched my cheek before he disappeared out the door.

I could feel myself hating what I had just done. Looking at my daughter I could imagine her distaste as well which didn't help. I dropped myself back into my seat and looked over to the books beside me.

I saw the title of Matt's book and I picked it back up again. Might as well try and give my hormones something since they seemed to be making bad decisions already. So I read through the chapters. Exploring the relationship between the two main characters and the back story. It was exciting but it was the sex scenes that showed Matt's talent.

They were creative and I couldn't help picturing the characters as the two of us. Feeling that thick length of his inside me again. Finding myself rubbing my thighs together as I kept reading.

My phone shouted out my horrible ringtone just as the characters were about to climax. Without thinking I answered the phone before regaining my breath. "Hello?"

"You okay? You sound out of breath."

"Hey, Matt." I gave my lips a little suck to stop the massive grin forming. "I was just reading your book."

"That good huh?"

I swallowed and felt my cheeks go red. "I guess."

"You guess? Well, thanks for the criticism."

"I didn't mean it like that."

I heard his chuckle down the line. "I know."

"How are you?"

"Still recovering from my shock last night."

"It was a great night." My hormones encouraged me to smile at the thought. Licking my lips I looked at the door and remembered the young doctor. Thought about how bad I felt at what I did.

"I'm still doing research tonight if you wanted another great surprise."

"Maybe." Biting my lip, thinking about the doctor. But then the memories of me and Matt came

BARTOND

flooding back. My hormones distracting me from my guilt.

"You wouldn't regret it. Plus I would love a female point of view. Help me with my writing."

Sighing softly. "Well if you need my help that badly. I can't say no."

"Good. And it's not just that I need you there. I want you there with me. It'll be fun. I guarantee it."

"I'll hold you to that." Fingers playing with the corner of the book as my imagination ran wild with what we could be getting up to tonight.

"Shall I pick you up from your apartment again?"

"Sounds good. What time?"

"Be ready for half seven. You can wear whatever you like tonight."

"No guidelines?"

"Clothing, no. All I will say is, keep an open mind." With that intriguing line he hung up. I could swear I heard him laughing as he did. So I put my phone down and carried on reading a few more chapters before getting up to head home. The plan was to have a shower. Curl my hair afterwards and find something casual but nice to wear. Something that would accent my cleavage. Give Matt something to look at whilst he was researching.

But before I went home I nipped into Kelly's room. She was awake and gave me a half smile as I entered. "Hey." Her voice was croaky but she looked better. The swelling had gone down quite a bit but she was still black and blue.

As I came to her side she tried to sit up but the pain she felt stopped her. "This is such a stupid question but how are you doing?"

"Oh god, I asked you that so many times. It's not now that I agree with you. It is a stupid question." Kelly tried to laugh but she just managed a crooked smile. "I'm doing fine. The doctor says I will make a full recovery. And when I do I'm going to grab a bat and smash that guy's head in."

I laughed suddenly. "You can't do that and you know it."

"But it is fun to fantasize about it."

"Did you give the police his name and stuff?"

"Of course I did. He's probably already in jail. Can you pass me some water?"

"Sure." I walked over to the jug and poured out a cup for her, sticking a straw in it. "Here you go."

"Thanks." She managed a few sips before setting it down on the table. "So what have you been up to without my supervision?"

"Supervision? You make it seem like you're the more responsible one."

"I am. If you think differently you need to get your head checked out." We both laughed. "Come on. I need details. Getting bored in this bed."

"If you're getting bored then read this. It's very good."

She took Matt's book from my fingers and smiled. "This wouldn't be written by your new friend, would it?"

"I just finished it in under a day. You won't be

disappointed."

"Okay. You get out of here. I know you have a life now so go live it. You don't need another hospital room in your life."

"I'll be coming back to check up on you. Don't worry about that. But I am off out tonight so I need to shower."

"Have fun." She winked at me before I kissed her forehead and left. Passing by the cafeteria I was looking forward to finding out what was in store for me tonight but a voice cut through my thoughts.

I turned and looked between the tables and saw a hand waving. As I got closer I noticed it was Greg. He was smiling at me which just made me feel worse that I was about to run out to meet Matt. To do god knows what together. "Look, about earlier. Sorry I reacted that way. Please sit down."

I checked the clock on the wall quickly and decided I had a little time to chat. "Okay." I sat opposite him. "You don't have apologise. I don't know what came over me. Don't worry about it."

"But I do worry. It's a curse really. So I sorted this all out." Just then the lights went out apart from the odd one or two and people started walking out of the kitchen door carrying plates.

I watched them dancing around with the food, placing it on a spare table next to us as they circled around. "I thought I'd bring us a meal whilst I had some spare time from my shift. I couldn't leave the building since I'm on call again but I figured this was second best."

"It looks great." I wasn't lying. The food looked better than the usual stuff they served here. "Do I just help myself?"

"Yeah. Dig in." Greg grabbed a plate and started filling it up with food. So I joined him and did the same. It wasn't like the fancy restaurant Matt took me to but this was just as good on so many different levels.

And we sat and ate our food. Spending time together, chatting about the random things that came to our minds. "So how did you manage to organise this? I've had the food here and it's nothing like this."

"I did have to bribe the kitchen staff to cook food I had delivered from the supermarket."

"You went to all that trouble?"

"You're worth the extra effort."

I flashed him a smile before scoffing down the amazing chicken he brought. "You're sweet."

"Sometimes." He shot me a wink before dessert was carted out. "Oh, you have a choice from three different desserts. Two are cheesecake and the other is some kind of sundae cup thing."

I looked across the trolley and took in the delicious food. The cheesecakes looked good but the little cups had me salivating. So I picked one up and started digging in with my spoon before Greg had even moved.

I caught his stare half-way through a mouthful and spoke without thinking, "What?" My hand shot up to stop the ice cream from falling out. Swallowing it was the wrong decision as my throat turned to ice.

"Oh my god, that's so cold."

Greg started laughing at me. "You really are something."

"Yeah. I bet you're counting your lucky stars at the moment, aren't you."

I didn't get an immediate response from him. Instead he simply looked at me smiling. Finally answering, "Yes I am."

I smiled back, my heart melting at his comment. "You're too sweet. You know that?"

"I've been told a few times. Continue eating your dessert, sorry to have interrupted you." I stuck my tongue out at him but I did what he said. Finishing off my cup and even going back for another.

We finished our dessert without a word. He allowed me to enjoy the taste of it and even enjoy a few looks from him. He truly held my heart with a tight grip at the moment and it was getting tighter.

The kitchen staff came back out when our plates were empty and took them away, clearing the desserts that we hadn't touched. It was almost like being at an actual restaurant. Greg wiped his mouth and then looked into my eyes. "So, how about we find a quiet part of the hospital so indulge in some more dessert?"

"Well." I looked down at my phone to see what the time was and my heart sank inside my chest. Opening my mouth to come up with an excuse but Greg took my hand and slipped me from the table.

I kept my mouth shut as he led me away from our little dinner. Keeping my mouth shut as he led the way. Following corridors whilst my brain was yelling at me to say something. To stop what was about to happen. Only my lips wouldn't move.

Getting tugged through a door and finding myself in a small room with a couple of bunk beds against the wall. Feeling the door against my back as Greg pounced on me. His hands running over my body. Eagerly cupping and grabbing. So fast I couldn't tell where they were which wasn't the best feeling.

Adding to the knot in my stomach as he kept moving. Dropping down to his knees in front of me. "Greg." My hand pressing to his head but that didn't seem to stop him. Feeling my bottoms loosening around my waist and then the cool air hitting my legs.

My knickers were gone in the next second and his hot breath kissed against my mound. Gasping a little at the sudden press of something wet. Parting me open and I couldn't stop the moan escaping my lips.

Shutting my eyes, telling myself to stop this but it was no good. My mind was starting to melt as my arousal peaked as his tongue explored. My head still on his head but my fingers curled into his hair to pull him close. Making sure he didn't stray from where his tongue was.

Feeling my thighs shaking a little as it probed that tightness. Closing my eyes and letting my head rest against the door. Willing my body to react to his touch. My pleasure flicking over my nerves like electricity. My hips pushing forward. Rolling in circles. Grinding on his face as I can't help it. Not able to be still.

A moan coming from me as is tongue ran up and pressed over that swollen button. Breath hitching in my throat as it flicked it. Feeling him smacking that tongue on it over and over. Teeth digging into my bottom lip as I finally opened my eyes and looked down at him.

His face between my thighs. Only now noticing how his fingers dug into my thighs. Feeling his want for my release and I needed it as well. Staring, blinking. Pleasure jolting through my body as his tongue didn't let up.

Thighs tensing, stomach clenching tight as I shook forwards. Pushing onto his wet touch. Needing it more and more as that pleasure built so quickly. Then his tongue shifted and started sliding down.

I grabbed his hair in my fingers and guided him back to where he was. Grinding my pussy to that tongue again, needing my clit to be attacked which he obliged. Mouth hanging open, pants coming quicker. Feeling the pleasure coming through every nerve.

My fingers holding him there making he didn't move from that spot. Thighs shaking so hard I could feel my legs threatening to give way. Leaning back to the door as that pleasure built so fast.

Biting into my bottom lip so I didn't alert the hospital workers what was going on when my orgasm hit. My wetness covering his mouth and tongue as I came for him. Giving him that taste, that honey. My tits heaving as I sucked in breaths through my fingers.

Those shakes slowly fading and I had to push

his face away to stop that tongue. Removing my hand and sucking in a deep breath. Steadying myself against the door. Looking down as he licked his lips. Looking so proud of himself.

Letting out a shaky breath as I quickly pulled up my bottoms. Covering myself, feeling my knickers sticking over those lips. His triumphant look disappearing quickly. "Is something wrong?"

"No. I just..." Blowing out a long sigh. "I have to go."

"Go? Was I that bad?"

"God no. The meal was great and this was....great also. Was really sweet of you and it has gotten you plenty of brownie points. But tonight I made plans with a friend."

"Oh? Anyone I know?" Greg stood up, my eyes shifting around the room so I didn't have to look at him.

"No. He's relatively new. Met him here at the hospital actually. His sister had just died."

"So you became friends with him?" Seeing his expression mixing confusion with sadness.

"Sort of. It's hard to explain. Matt needed someone to chat to and I knew what it was like to lose someone." I shuffled my hands nervously as Greg stared at me. "Do you have a problem with me having friends?"

"No." He gave a stern answer but I could tell he wasn't okay with it. The last few days had been great fun but now I was reminded of a bad part of any relationship. Jealousy.

"Look, Greg. We've been out on one date."

"Two now."

Greg cut me off but I ignored it. "We had sex and it was amazing but we never said we were exclusive. So I don't think you have the right to be upset about me having a guy friend." I tried to keep my tone friendly and calm but the anger I suddenly felt didn't work with that idea.

"Okay, I'm sorry." Greg pulled the door open making me shift out of the way so I wasn't hit. Following him into the hallway. "I can't help the way I feel but you're right. There was no need or right for me to get like that. I'm sorry."

"It's fine." Looking at his face I could tell he was sorry but that wasn't good enough. That feeling I had deep down inside was building and I couldn't stop it. The way he reacted had me thinking I was doing something wrong.

I knew I had fucked Matt but like I had said me and Greg weren't exclusive. There would be no right for me to be angry if he did the same. So he wasn't allowed to be either. I tried to blow out my frustration but it stuck around.

"I should get going otherwise I'm going to be late."

"Yeah, of course." I was quickly pulled around and into a tight hug. I wrapped my arms around him but they were limp. When he let go I jumped onto tip-toes and kissed his cheek. "Call me when you get in?"

"Sure." I didn't particularly like the way he was being so clingy now. All I did was tell him I had a guy friend and all of a sudden he changed. Gone was the charming young man who managed to get me into bed on the first date.

Now he was acting more his age and acting like a little child who had his cookie stolen by another boy. But I couldn't deal with it right now. Any more if this act and I would be fuming steam from my ears.

"I'll let you know when I get home."

"Good." The doctor took a step next to me. "Can I walk you to the bus?"

He gave me a pleading look but I shot it down quickly. "I'm in a bit of a rush. Already running late. But the food was amazing and it was a sweet surprise. Honestly." I kissed his lips but pulled away when he pushed forward for another. "Have to run."

Turning my back on him so I couldn't see that hurt look on his face and I walked out of the hospital. Grabbing a bus as it came by. Sitting down, trying to shift that guilt. Not feeling like helping with research any more.

However I didn't want to go back to the apartment either. So instead I climbed off at the next stop and walked around the city centre. It was that time between the day and the night.

I could hear the music from the various pubs and nightclubs as they started getting lively. I came up to a bench and sat down. As my jeans tightened around my thighs I felt my phone vibrating. It was a message from Matt asking where I was and if I was okay. Instead of replying through text I dialled his number and smiled when he answered. "Hey, you."

"Hi. Sorry about tonight."

"Why do I sense you're phoning to say sorry about not being at your apartment?"

"Because you would be right. I'm not really up for helping with your research tonight. Had a fight and I'm not in the mood."

There was a long pause before he answered. "Look, I just cancelled my plans. Where are you?"

"You don't have to do that."

"Too late. It's done and I can't undo it. Where are you?"

I looked around me and saw a neon sign across the green in front of me for a pub. "I'm near a place in the city centre called The Lounge. Do you know it?"

"I don't but I'm fluent in Google. I'll be there as soon as I can. First round is on me."

There was no point in arguing with him so I simply gave a noise in response and put my phone back into my pocket. Waiting for a few more minutes before getting up and heading inside.

There was no bouncer so I simply walked in and straight up to the bar. Before the bartender got to me I was planning on ordering a simple water but when he finally arrived I asked for a shot of Sambuca and a beer instead.

The shot disappeared very quickly and I started on the beer. Before it was all gone another shot was taken and I ordered another beer when the first was empty. Turning around with my replenished alcohol I looked around for Matt. Only I couldn't see his face anywhere.

One face I did see was the jock I had bumped into leaving Kelly's apartment. The guy who had beaten her into a black and blue mess. The anger I had felt from Greg's childish attitude seemed so insignificant compared to what I felt now. My skin raged with heat as I looked at his face.

He was smiling and laughing with his friends. Having a good time whilst Kelly was laid up in hospital looking the way she did. My hand clenched the beer bottle so hard my knuckles turned white. Feeling the nails on my other hand digging in sharp but barely registering the pain.

Then he looked directly at me. He must have recognised me because he pulled a sickening smirk before carrying on with his laughter. I couldn't take looking at him any more. Slamming the bottle down on the bar I stormed through the crowd. Nudging past people bigger than me I finally came face to face with the jock.

I didn't even think about my actions. Ramming my fists against his chest I tried to push him back but it didn't work. He was just too large and too heavy. But when he laughed in response to my attempt it brought out even more rage.

Before I knew it my hand was balling into a fist and I flung it at his face. The pain I felt was unbearable when I connected but I revelled in the fact he definitely felt it worse. This time it was me who was laughing as he groaned in pain. A hand held up to his mouth.

And it felt even better when he removed it and I

saw the busted up lip. But then the mood changed and I saw the look in his eyes. It couldn't have been classed as anger. The way it looked was beyond that.

His large frame moved forwards and I took a step back but I hit into someone. A sick grin twisted his lips and I saw his large hand being pulled back. I couldn't believe what was about to happen. I was going to end up in hospital right next to Kelly.

So I shut my eyes and waited for that large fist to come smashing into my face. Wondering how painful it would be. I felt a whoosh of air and skin slapping skin but no pain. So I shot my eyes open and saw a man standing to my side. His fist had stopped the punch just inches from me.

After blinking a few times at disbelief I looked up at my knight in shining armour. Just as he threw the jocks punch back I saw his great smile. It was Matt. Turning up just in time to save me.

I went to thank him but the student threw another punch. Only it was no good. Matt twisted so the punch sailed past his shoulder and threw one of his own. It was only one and it didn't seem that hard but when it hit this jock's throat he went down like a bag of bricks.

His friends stood forward but the look Matt gave them had them standing down. So they grabbed their injured buddy and ran out the pub, pushing people aside as they rushed. Then Matt finally turned around and I thanked him with a big hug.

After a few seconds he pushed me back a few inches and stared into my eyes with worry. A hand coming up to cup my cheek. "Picking fights with bigger guys generally isn't a good idea. Especially for someone so tiny."

"I know it wasn't a good idea but he attacked my room-mate. She's in hospital because of him and he's walking around laughing." My voice rising as I felt the anger again.

"What!? If I knew that I wouldn't have just thrown one punch."

"No. What you did was perfect. The police are looking for him anyway. He'll be locked up before the nights out hopefully."

"Hopefully." His hands gripped my hips as he stared down at me. Sniffing the air. "Have you been doing Sambuca shots?"

"Only two." With that confident statement my left leg gave way and I stumbled. "I swear. I'm not drunk."

"You had a lot more than that last night." I shook my head slowly as I looked up into his deep eyes. "Maybe we should sit down and have some water."

"But I want to keep drinking." Standing up and straightening my legs. "I think you should join me."

"I think you should get some air. Come with me." He curled me into an arm and started leading me towards the front of the pub. Once the cool air hit me I felt a little worse to start off with. But then I saw the blue and red flashing lights of a police car.

I squinted as they shone in my eyes but I could make out the large figure of the jock pressed against the metal work. Arms pulled back in cuffs. I smiled and a weird drunken cackle came out of my mouth. Hearing Matt laughing with me. "Looks like they caught him after all. You know I think your brawl brought the cops. You should feel good about yourself."

I punched him in the ribs a little harder than I expected. A whoosh of unexpected air came out of his lungs. "Oh, sorry. But you should be ready for a punch from a drunken chick."

"I guess so." Matt gently tugged me away from the wonderful scene and towards the taxi rank down the road. I was put into a taxi and was happy when Matt climbed in next to me. So I snuggled up to him as he gave the driver my address. Pushing my shoulder against his ribs I purred as an arm came around my shoulders and pulled me even closer.

And that's the way I stayed, tucked under his arm all the way to my apartment. Feeling comfortable and safe. The world swinging around as he pulled me out and scooped me up. My head feeling heavy, curling my arms around his neck. Being carried up the stairs to the right floor.

My hand was too unstable to get the key into the lock so he did that for me. Carrying me over to the sofa he placed me down. I followed his walk as he took off his jacket and hung it on the peg.

Then he walked into the kitchen and grabbed me a glass of water. It was sat down onto the coffee table and then he looked down at me. "DVDs?"

"That way." My arm drunkenly swung towards Kelly's room.

"Are you sure I'm allowed in there?"

I giggled at his smirk. "I'll give you a one time pass to the bedroom." Matt disappeared and came back with a case in his hands. Squinting as I tried to spot the cover. "Which one did you pick?"

"You'll have to wait and see." It was loaded up into the player and he came back over to the sofa. His body slipped down beside me and I rested my head onto his lap. The fabric of his trousers felt better than the cushion.

I twisted my body and looked up at him. When his eyes came down to mine I smiled. "You're very good at looking after a drunk person."

"I've had a lot of practice in the past. My ex-wife used to be quite the party animal. Was always looking after her when she got home, barely able to walk."

"You're a very sweet man."

There was a sadness in his eyes after talking about his ex-wife. "Thank you. Now sip your water and enjoy the movie."

"Yes, sir." I took a sip and rested my head back down on his leg. Only I didn't enjoy the movie. I lasted about five minutes before my eyes were too heavy to keep open thanks to his fingers combing through my hair. There were worse ways to fall asleep than having Matt looking after me.

I found myself thinking that he was such a sweetheart looking after me like this. Not only did he have the body and the knowledge on how to use it, he had this other side to him. Plus he wasn't a young man who would get jealous at the first sign of another male.

Chapter 6

When I awoke I blessed the glass of water Matt had given me. My head had a little ache but felt surprisingly good. "Matt?" I didn't get an answer and when I looked around the apartment I didn't see any sign he had even stayed.

Bread was put into the toaster and I spread butter over my breakfast. When I returned to the sofa with my cup of coffee and the food I sat on a piece of paper. Lifting one cheek I plucked it out from underneath me.

Matt had left a note telling me he enjoyed last night but I owed him. It told me to be ready for a party tonight at five. And to not be late this time. He had drawn a smiley face at the bottom with a thumbs up.

Folding the note I left it on my coffee table whilst I ate and drank my breakfast. Forgetting a shower since I would have one later before the party. So I changed my clothes for something comfier. Then got to work where I spent most of my time helping students with their coursework and starting Matt's second book.

By the time I had finished my shift at the library, I had almost finished it. And I would have done if my boss hadn't told me to leave at the end of my shift. So I took it with me when I left for the hospital.

Since it was nice and sunny I walked the whole way with a smile on my face. I couldn't believe how good I felt today considering all it took was two shots and one beer to get me too drunk to stay awake last night.

When I arrived at the hospital, I quickly popped my head in to see my daughter. Gave her forehead the usual kiss and then made my way to Kelly's room. She was reading a magazine but put it down when I walked in. "Hey, you."

"You sound a lot better. Look it as well."

"I feel better as well. Went for a little walk earlier today. Couldn't stand being in bed any longer."

"How did it feel?"

"Fine until my ribs started aching with every breath."

"Ouch." I took a seat next to the bed and placed the book on the table. "I have some good news that will cheer you up. The police have the guy."

"Yeah? How did you find out before me?"

"I was there when he was arrested." Her forehead creased up with confusion. "I went out for a few drinks after having a little fight with Greg. I saw that jock in the bar and drunkenly started a fight with him."

"You did what?!" She tried to sit up suddenly but fell back holding her side.

"Look. Don't worry. He didn't lay a finger on

me. He tried but Matt stepped in and knocked him down with one punch."

"Just one?" Kelly sat up slower this time, positioning her pillow to allow her to stay in this position. "That boy is a large hulk and he knocked him down in one punch?"

"Yep."

"Clearly I need to give this Matt fellow my thanks."

"He was great. Even looked after me since I got way too drunk."

"You didn't go onto the shots did you?"

"Pretty much as soon as I walked in." She giggled at me. "I wasn't feeling too great."

"Tell me what happened. What did the doctor do?"

I leant forwards in the chair and looked into her eyes as she got a little more comfortable. "It starts off with me having plans with Matt."

"The other hot guy."

"Yes. The other hot guy in my life." Laughing as I shook my head.

"And you two are just friends? Just so I know what the story is."

I could see the expression of disbelief. "Maybe that's a story for another time."

"I sense that is going to be an interesting story."

"Anyway, carrying on. On my way out of the hospital Greg had set up a meal for us in the cafeteria. He had brought in food from the supermarket and paid the chefs to cook it. They brought it all out on trolleys and it was divine. And it was so sweet of him to do it."

"So what was the problem?"

"He asked me if I wanted to sneak off and have some dessert. Only I told him I had plans with a friend. Then when he found out the friend was male, he started acting all jealous. I haven't dated someone in so long I had forgotten all the great feelings you get. But I had also forgot how annoyed I get when someone acts jealous. You remember how my ex-husband used to be. And the doctor went from being a cute young guy to being a jealous little boy."

"I can see his point of view though. However maybe acting jealous wasn't his best move. You've only been on one date, haven't you?"

"Exactly. There hasn't been any talk about us labelling the relationship or anything. So for me it came out of nowhere. And the more I thought about it the more I got annoyed and then I got to the bar and started drinking. The events just happened after that."

"So what did you and Matt get up to after the fight?"

I pulled a face at her. "Nothing naughty. He was actually a real gentleman. Matt took me home. He made sure I had a glass of water. I laid my head on his lap whilst we watched a movie. Well, he watched it, I fell asleep with him stroking his fingertips through my hair."

"Wow. Sounds like the kind of guy you need to keep a hold of."

"Shut it. He's just a friend who maybe I fooled around with once."

"What!? Why didn't you lead with that story?"

"Because I don't kiss and tell."

"Oh come on. I'm stuck in this bed. I can't have fun of my own. You need to give me something juicy."

"Fine. Since you're so interested in my sex life." So I recalled back the memory of me and Matt in Marie's private room. As I told her what happened, maybe in a little more detail than needed, I found my breathing becoming heavier. That tingling feeling between my thighs was obvious after I had finished.

God, all I could think about was having Matt again. I think Kelly was thinking the same judging by her expression. Just as my story was finished a nurse came walking in with a tray of food for Kelly.

"I'll leave and let you get something to eat. Head down to see my daughter for a bit before going out."

"Matt again?"

"Shut it. Eat your food before I throw some at you."

"You wouldn't dare. I'm a defenceless injured woman."

"All I see is my cocky room-mate. With a bit of added colour."

"I would call you something horrible if the nurse wasn't here." The hospital worker smiled and quickly left the room with a nervous look. "You scared her off."

"I think that was you. And she's stuck with you.

I on the other hand can leave."

"You'll be stuck with me when I get out of here. I'll make sure of it. Me, you and Matt."

If something had been in arms reach I would have chucked it at her. "Watch it otherwise I'll decorate your room pink"

"Don't you dare!"

"Then zip it about, Matt. Eat your jelly."

"I will." She gave me a wink before I left the room and made my way down to the next floor. As I entered the room I bumped into the back of a white coat. "Sorry. Wasn't looking where I was going."

"It's fine, Louise."

The sound of my name made me look up at the eyes peering down at me. "Hey, Greg." I dipped my head back down and scooted around him. "How's my baby doing?"

"I'm doing great." I looked back over my shoulder at his grin. "Too soon?"

And then I burst out laughing. Unable to keep myself silent. "Very funny, Greg. Glad to see you are in a better mood."

"I would apologise but honestly I just want to forget how I acted and remember the amazing meal we had."

"That sounds like a good idea to me." I walked forward and placed a gentle kiss against his lips. I was planning on that being that but when his arm snared me I was yanked into a deeper kiss.

And in his arms I melted. Pushing my mouth against his as my own arms curled around his neck.

132

I felt his tongue probe so I sucked on it. Letting it play with mine as I arched my back, letting my curves brush against him.

I smiled when I heard a soft moan come from his lips. Pulling back from him I opened my eyes to see his. "Well I think that means we've made up?"

"Don't get cocky, Greg. But maybe." I gave him a grin before turning and pecking my daughter on her forehead.

"So how about tonight?"

"Tonight?"

"I'll make everything up to you with one huge night of….. dessert."

Now I was stuck in a predicament. I could tell him the truth that I had plans to go out with Matt. Only, wouldn't that bring the same predicament as yesterday. The one that had me getting angry at his behaviour. "I don't think I can do tonight."

There was a sudden sadness to his eyes. "Plans again?"

My mouth opened to say yes, only what came out was instead a lie. "Actually, the police need another statement from me. Last night I saw the guy who had attacked Kelly. Called the police and they got him. They just need a statement so there isn't any loop hole for him to escape through."

"Well I can't keep you from that. That guy deserves to rot in jail doing that to a woman. Such a creep."

"I know. So I'll take a rain-check on that dessert." I reached up on tip-toes and kissed his cheek.

"I should get going. Hope they don't have me there for too long."

"The police can be troublesome with their time keeping. I've had to give statements a few times."

"Some rough moments from your youth?"

The smile that shone down upon me held something about my comment of his youth. "In the case of domestic abuse and a few other cases here in the hospital. Bullet wounds, that kind of thing."

"And your youth?" Greg simply showed that smile again. "Okay, keep your mouth shut. I'll get it out of you sooner or later."

"I doubt that but feel free to give it a try. Perhaps try blackmail. I'm susceptible to a naked woman." I got a peck back and Greg left the room. The clock above my daughter's bed showed I didn't have to be ready for Matt's party for a little while. However I couldn't wait around the hospital just in case Greg saw me.

So I left and made my way back to the apartment. Whilst there I managed to get the place cleaned up, washing done. I even picked out a sexy little black dress. The only problem was it wasn't mine. Kelly always said she never had a problem with me borrowing her clothes but this was her favourite.

I slipped it on and any worries I had of her finding out slid from my mind as I checked myself in the mirror. The material hugged my curves but wasn't too tight around my belly. Enough room to breathe whilst giving the guys a hard time to keep their eyes to themselves.

I liked it and refused to take it off for the remainder of my waiting time. Which meant cleaning went at half speed just in case I got something on it. Once the place was tidy I decided to sit down and have a glass of wine.

I was half-way through the deep red before the buzzer went. Matt was let in and his face when he saw me was a picture I wish I had a camera to capture. "I'm guessing I look good then."

"You do indeed. So good I'm thinking about blowing off this party."

"You can't do that. I've been looking forward to it all day."

"I would hate to disappoint you."

"Good." My eyes left his stunning features and looked at what he was wearing. Blue faded jeans and an old looking t-shirt. Despite the fact he looked good in them I was a little confused. "I feel very over-dressed at the moment."

Matt stepped forward with a glint of mischief in his eyes. "Well there's one way we could change that." His body brushed against mine. Towering over me with that grin and I felt my breath catch in my throat before it quickened. "All it would take is the drop of your zip." His hand curled around my waist, sliding up my back where the zip sat. His fingertips such a delicious touch through the material.

"But then we would miss the party." I stared into his eyes which seemed to be filled with an ocean of lust. So I arched my back. Pressing myself against his chest and I saw the flicker of desire in his pupils grow. Lifting up a hand I let my fingertips move over his chest. Feeling the way his muscles defined his body.

Tucking a finger into the waist line of his jeans I tugged him forward. Pressing my lips up to his. Within a second of our mouths meeting I was pulled in tightly. Arms around me, holding me to him as our kiss exploded into passion.

Our tongues met and danced as our lips moulded to each other's. I tried to moan, to show my approval of his touch but it came out as a sigh of air that was swallowed by his lips.

Feeling my breath catch when he pulled back suddenly. Despite still being in his arms I felt colder. Our heavy breathing mixing our breaths together as I looked up at him. There was no way for me to behave around this man. Like something in him called to that part of me. The feeling of being lost in passion with him had my heart pounding. Increasing the dampness between my thighs. I could feel my knickers clinging to me.

Dragging my hand up over his chest I let my thumb follow the line of his jaw. Then he smiled and it had my lips following the same movement. "Do you think we should get to the party?"

His words came out as a whisper of control. "Sure." As his arms slipped from around me I quickly pushed myself on tip-toes and pecked his lips.

We made our way down to where his car was waiting at the curb. "So where is this party?"

"It's a surprise. One I'm sure you'll love."

"It's a good thing I trust you." I climbed in and moaned at the way the soft seats cradled me. Almost like being in Matt's arms. The engine roared loudly and he drove us through the city. "So how come I'm all dressed up and you're wearing that?"

"You don't think I look good in jeans and a t-shirt?"

"I do but that's the second time you've dodged the question."

"I'm just trying to figure out how much to tell you."

"Intriguing." I looked over at him and then quickly jabbed his ribs with a finger.

"Ow. What are you doing?" He giggled as he kept his eyes on the road.

"I'm going to keep prodding you until you tell me why." I jabbed him again which made him giggle more. I knew I was hurting him and that was the point. It was playful and yet, I knew it would make him tell me. No one enjoyed being jabbed in the ribs. So I poked him again.

Matt burst out laughing and I was just able to make out the words, "Fine. I'll tell you."

"Wise man."

"You have a mean streak and I'm not just talking about your punching last night."

"Just remember that in the future."

Matt laughed as he meandered through traffic. "The reason I'm wearing this is because I get clothes at the party."

"Oh? And why is that?"

He looked over at me and I showed him my fingertip again, threatening to attack. "Because it is a theme party. The women getting waited on by the men. We get our uniforms upon arrival. And I'm not saying any more than that because it will spoil the surprise. No matter how many times you jab me."

I looked at him and decided to leave it there. My curiosity had been sated and I didn't want to ruin any more surprises. I was now even more interested about the party. So I stayed quiet for the rest of the journey. Letting my eyes move over the scenery as we left the city. Finding my stare moving over Matt as he drove. He might have been looking casual but it was a great look.

Soon we pulled off the road and onto a driveway that seemed to stretch on for ages. The gravel crackled under the tyres as we crept between the lines of trees. Following the path like a boat on a river. Pulling into an empty space at the front of the house. Only it looked more like a mansion. A round fountain with three tiers of stone was spouting clear water in the middle of the courtyard.

Two lines of parked vehicles ran either side where the gravel met dark green grass. Most of them were even flashier than Matt's. The one next to us looked more like a spaceship than a car. The bonnet was made of a clear material showing off the shiny, expensive engine underneath. Just one of the seats looked like it could sort out the bills for Kelly's apartment for the whole year.

We both climbed out and started making our

way up the many steps to the thick oak doors. Seeing our reflection in the window I giggled suddenly. As the door opened he nudged me. I spotted his smile in the corner of my eye.

A tall, skinny woman came walking towards us. Her long brunette hair was too long to not be hair extensions. Shockingly white teeth shining through her smile. "Hey, Matt."

"Jenny." The heels on her feet clicked over the stone as she reached up and hugged him. I saw the way she arched her back and pressed to him. The hug seemed friendly and yet held something more. Like they had been intimate with each other. Or maybe it had been something more than that.

Jenny pulled away but kept a hand hooked around his shoulder. "What have you brought with you?"

"He's brought Louise."

Her eyes moved over me. A look of innocence but somehow I felt like I was being weighed up to go in to the meat grinder. Then a Cheshire cat of a grin appeared. "She's cute. Does she know the rules?"

"Rules?"

"She's fine. Shall we take this inside?"

"Let's." Jenny left Matt and hooked an arm through mine. "Don't worry, cutie. I'll look after you."

"Thanks." I didn't know if my voice sounded shaky or if it was just in my head. Jenny led me through the large oak doors with Matt following closely. My heels tapped over the concrete and onto marble flooring. Black with white veins running through it. Any wood I could see was dark, almost black.

Sitting to my left was a large door and then next to that was a table. It was so long it wouldn't have been out of place in a castle where the occupants would have to shout at each other to pass the salt.

Lines and lines of eye masks sat on top. Some were lace and didn't look like they would cover much. Others were white porcelain. Tear drops marked some of the smooth cheeks. Others had feathers and flowers attached.

Jenny's voice snapped me out of my trance. "Which one do you like the look of?"

"Umm...." I lowered my fingers and let them slide over the porcelain ones. Thinking about the opera musical about the phantom.

"Go for a black one." Matt whispered into my ear which got him a slap around the arm. "Hey."

"You know the rules, scuff. You can't see the mask being picked. Now get going and get out of those horrible clothes."

"Like I'm going to leave my best clothes here with you around." He winked at us both before disappearing through a swinging door. Beyond it was just a corridor which he walked down.

Jenny's finger traced down my forearm. "So which one will you pick?"

"What kind of party is this?"

Her curiosity seemed to spike, "What did Matt tell you?"

"Clearly not enough."

"Clearly. How open are you, sexually?"

Her bluntness took me by surprise. "Um... I don't know. Haven't really thought about it."

I watched her looking into my eyes. Her tongue slipped out across her bottom lip. "Tell you what. If at any point you want to leave. Want it to stop. We have a safe word, balloon."

"Balloon?"

"Yes. It might seem odd but you'd be surprised some of the stuff that gets screamed out at my parties."

"Oh?" I wanted to ask her what they were but I decided against it. "Balloon."

"You say that and you will be gently escorted to this room. Here, you can take a seat and chill out. You can decide to come back in if you want to but you must be wearing your mask. Or you can leave."

"I came with Matt."

"I shall get a hold of him if I'm not otherwise engaged. But you seem like the kind of girl who enjoys a good party."

Blushing with a smile. "I guess we'll find out."

"That's the spirit." A voice came from behind me but I didn't turn. Jenny pecked me on the cheek and walked off to attend to whoever it was. My eyes moved over the many masks they had. I leaned towards the black ones, knowing they will go well with my dress.

Sitting at the front was a pretty one made from plastic. The main shape was of a butterfly, the left wings bigger than the right. The eye holes were surrounded by smaller ones. Lifting it up I slipped the band around my head. I stood there breathing in and out. Wondering what exactly I was doing.

I didn't know these people. I didn't even know Matt all that well either. But I had jumped on him at that club. Didn't even hesitate. I felt fingers gripping my arms and I breathed in smelling Jenny's alluring scent. It filled my nostrils and had me wondering if it was perfume or just her natural smell.

I was pulled to the side and my eyes caught my reflection in the mirror. Jenny appeared beside me. "Very sexy. It's one of my personal favourites."

"I'm sorry. Did you want to wear it?"

"Oh please. I have plenty more to wear. And it looks very nice on you."

"Thank you." For a few more seconds she stood there looking at me. Eyes meeting mine. "What?"

"How well do you know, Matt?"

"Probably not as well as I think."

"Remember that. Wouldn't want you getting hurt."

"What do you mean?" Jenny opened her mouth but was called for. I tried to get her attention back but she walked off.

I stood staring at myself, questioning my reflection. "What are you doing here? You have no idea where you are with no way of getting home." Jenny had me wondering who Matt was. I knew he had to do research for his kind of books but this seems a little more than that. What kind of party had he brought me to?

Turning around I was about to excuse myself from the large house and wait outside. Only Jenny had donned a mask of her own. Her fingers gripped my wrist before I could speak and I was walked through a pair of mirrored door. My heart feeling like it would burst out of my chest.

They slowly opened and I saw the impressive room on the other side. It was huge. Golden chandeliers hung from the ceiling. Three of them shining light through expensive crystals.

Chaise loungers and sofas were dotted around the room. So many women in here. Dressed so smartly and a few of them showing a lot more skin than I was. They didn't pay much attention to me but they all smiled at Jenny.

My eyes looked around at them all trying to distinguish who they were but they had masks on. Just their eyes and lips were visible. It was like I had walked into an old fashioned novel.

Jenny steered me towards the bar in the corner. Sliding behind it she didn't ask if I wanted anything. She poured two glasses of champagne and slid one over. "To calm your nerves." I didn't question it, just grabbed the glass and downed the liquid. It felt like velvet sliding down my throat.

The barmaid poured me another but held her fingers on the bottom. "This is expensive stuff. Slow down otherwise you'll pass out."

"Sorry. Nervous."

"I can tell." As her fingers left the glass they wrapped around mine. "Just remember the safe word.

And above all, have fun. Just remind yourself that this is a safe place. You never have to do anything you don't want to." She pulled such a warm smile. It made me not want to leave her side for the whole night.

And just as I thought that she walked off towards a small stage. It was just big enough for her to stand on. As she raised her glass of champagne so did the others. I joined in, not wanting to be left out.

"Greetings to you all this evening and welcome to the fifteenth annual party at our grounds. This evening's proceedings are a little different this year. As you can see, the guys of our party have been taking away and you have no clue why. And if they have been good boys they have kept this information to themselves."

Her eyes scanned over the crowd and landed on me. And as she carried on, that's where they stayed. I couldn't help but look back at her. She looked like an empress ruling over her subjects up there.

"Now I shall reveal to you all where they have gone. They are currently all waiting in the kitchen with my husband. They have all been changed into something more fitting for their positions tonight and will soon be coming around with trays of drinks and other treats."

So far it didn't sound too bad. Being waited on by hunky men, especially when one of them was Matt. I wondered what kind of outfit they would be wearing. "Now, a party here wouldn't be complete with a little naughtiness. However this time it will be your choice when it happens and with who. You are in control tonight."

She took a sip of her champagne and grinned. "But if you are thinking about picking a particular guy tonight." Again her eyes came to me and I knew she meant Matt. "This may be a little more difficult than you think."

My gut twisted with uncertainty. Knowing Matt was here was the only thing keeping me calm. "When they come out and you pick your man. Just simply give them an erection. How you do this is up to you but if managed, the waiter will ask a simple question. Slave or master."

She paused for effect and the crowd was silent. I had so many questions to ask but everyone else was listening without a word. Smiling up at the host of these crazy parties. I screamed at myself to leave. Just to wait by Matt's car for this whole thing to be over.

"It is your decision if you are the slave or the master. However if you pick slave then you are open for whatever they decide to do. You all know the safe word but if you're like me, there's nothing more thrilling then being at the mercy of a man."

A few of the women cheered which brought out a grin from Jenny. "Now I believe I've teased you all enough. So let's bring out the boys." As she said this a man came walking through the door at the other end. He stood there, wearing tight black boxers and a bow tie. A mask covered most of his face and the rest of his modesty was gone.

My eyes moved over his toned figure and that gorgeous arse. I didn't know who this person was but something deep down inside my body was screaming for me to get to know him. But then the rest of them came walking through the open doorway.

All of them wearing the same outfit. Tight black boxers that left nothing to the imagination, a bow tie and a mask. Each of them different but all covering the identity of our waiters.

My eyes moved from one to the other as they kept filling up the room. Carrying shiny silver trays with flutes of champagne and little bowls of snacks. I tried to find Matt but it was hard. Blondes and the few with grey hair could be ignored but that still left just under half.

Most of them were the same build as Matt and the one thing I knew about him was the size of his member. Only I couldn't go round looking in their underwear. I could make a mistake and pick a guy who wasn't him.

So I stood and watched. At first none of the women did anything. Everyone was happily chatting, drinking. And it wasn't long before a waiter came walking towards me. So I looked him over. Brown hair. Body could have been put in a museum next to a plaque saying it was the best a man could look.

Looking lower I saw the package he held and it certainly could be the size of Matt's. But something was wrong with the way he walked. It wasn't him and when he spoke I was sure of it. "More champagne?"

I held up my still half-full glass and smiled. "No thank you. I'm all good for now."

"Please let me know if you change your mind."

The eyes of this stranger running down my body. "I love your titties."

I bit my lip to stop the laughter from erupting out at that boyish phrase. Seeing the hurt look as he turned and walked away. Breathing out that chuckle slowly before sipping on my drink. Eyes shifting back to the stage where I noticed Jenny with a twinkle in her eye.

Following her gaze I watched as a blonde woman wearing a white, almost see-through dress delved her hand into the underwear of a waiter. My heart skipped a beat until I saw the blonde hair. It wasn't Matt and I still had a small chance to find my safety.

But right now my eyes were transfixed on this woman. She was stroking the waiter's cock like it was the last one she would ever touch. And soon he was reacting to it, growing in her grasp like someone had turned a tap on his blood flow. I watched and felt my own body reacting to the public actions of this woman. Never had I seen something like this.

The waiter was massive and I found myself licking my lips as a tingle started forming between my thighs. I mouthed the word, wow to myself as the waiter asked his question. The woman cackled and shouted out, "I want to be a slave. Fuck me baby, anyway you want."

"With pleasure, miss." The motions of the waiter was slow as he laid his tray down on a small table next to the wall and then walked over to her with a stamp. He pressed the blue end to her wrist before suddenly ripping her dress open. I jumped at the suddenness of it all. Her underwear on show to the whole room and she didn't even care.

She was laughing and cheering as his hands moved over her body. His lips crashing against hers as she was hoisted up into the air. The waiter pressed her to the wall and I didn't even see how he did it but her knickers were swinging from her foot as he slid inside her so suddenly.

This blonde threw her head back and moaned like a wolf howling at the moon. Enjoying her experience as she was fucked in front of us all. As shocked as I was with the scene, many others were still chatting and flirting with the waiters like nothing was happening.

Of course there were some attracted to the scene. It was like they were watching a live porno. I could imagine them sitting there with popcorn, munching and cheering on the action as it happened.

It wasn't long before she was screaming about coming and the split second after, she did. Calling out how great his fucking was and how good she felt. And when she quietened down he still didn't stop. This waiter kept fucking and ramming his length inside her like there was no stopping him.

I yelped when Jenny suddenly appeared next to me. "Sorry." She laughed a little and watched the action. "I see you like the party so far."

"Huh?"

"The action. You seem to be concentrating on it very closely."

"I'm just a little shocked at how quick it happened."

"Yes. We do get some people here who just want to be fucked as many times as they can before the night is over."

"So this happens every year?"

"Well this year I made it a little special with the men as waiters. Usually it's the other way around. Every year we all get together and enjoy each other's company." A waiter came walking over and smiled at us both. "Let me introduce you to my husband, Steven."

"Husband?"

He grinned. "You seem shocked that Jenny is married?"

"Well. It's just the party."

"We get that a lot but we love each other very much."

"So you don't play with others?"

Jenny almost scoffed, "Of course we do. You don't see me giving him an erection do you?"

"Right. But how did you know it was him with the mask on?"

Jenny turned to Steven and looked up at him adoringly before turning back. "No one else can smile at me and make my heart skip like that."

I was tempted to say how cute that was but the comment was lost to what was happening in the room. "Sounds like you truly love each other."

"Like I said." Steven got a glass taken from his tray by Jenny and then he walked off to mingle.

"How can you stand sharing him with these women?"

"Call me a bad lady but I get so turned on seeing him please someone else. And he does in return."

"Really?"

"Yeah. At the end of the day I know he's coming to bed with me. And during the rest of the year we spend it together. Madly in love." Jenny looked at me whilst she sipped the bubbly liquid. "Are you telling me you don't find it a little exciting that you don't know these men? Well, apart from one."

"I don't know." My eyes moved across the room at the half naked men.

"That guy right there?" She pointed to the nearest waiter. He had grey hair but his body didn't match that ageing colour. "Look at the body. Don't you get excited thinking about it being yours? Think about his hands running over your body. His tongue touching you in places that make you shiver. Feeling his cock penetrating you."

I didn't notice my breathing getting heavy until Jenny giggled. Licking my suddenly dry lips I swallowed. "I guess so. But..."

Jenny looked at me and must have seen my apprehension. "Look. They are all wearing masks and it is very hard to tell these men apart. But I do know for a fact that Matt has a scar on his left arse cheek."

He does? I thought back to our night of fucking at Marie's but I never saw his bare arse. Just felt him behind me. "A scar?"

"Yep. And when tonight is over you should ask

him the story behind it. It's extremely hilarious."

"Thanks." And then she was gone. Moving through the crowd chatting with the waiters and the women. I hadn't noticed the sudden influx of nudity around the room.

People were fucking and tasting each other. The moans coming to my ears as I looked around. Then the grey waiter who had been close before was now facing me. I saw him coming closer so I quickly finished my champagne. I might know it wasn't Matt under that mask but what Jenny had said had my intrigue peaked.

My judgement wasn't as clear as it should be thanks to the champagne and the atmosphere. The waiter stopped and offered me a glass from his tray. "Refill?" His voice rolled off his tongue with an Irish accent.

"Why not." Smiling I took a glass and sip the alcohol. Then I looked down at his boxers. They were so tight I could see the outline of his cock. It wasn't huge but was very evident.

"See something you like?"

I looked up at him like a child who had been caught with her hand in the cookie jar. "Do you come to these parties every year?"

"I've been here for the last three. This is the first time I have had to give up my ability to choose."

"Oh? Not something you're into?"

"Not really but my wife comes to these things as well."

"What is she wearing?"

He looked over to the blonde who had been the first to pick a waiter. "Not anything any more."

"Oh. Do you mind her being fucked by other guys?" I thanked the champagne in my hand sarcastically for letting me be so blunt.

"It doesn't bother me. None of this really bothers me. It's just I don't want to be picked by some of these crazy women. I picked wrong last time and I still have scars from her bite marks."

I burst out giggling. "Really?"

"Yep." He lifted his arm and on his tricep were those teeth marks.

"Wow. She must have thought you looked good enough to eat."

The silver fox laughed. "Usually that would sound good to me but not that time."

"So now you're afraid you are going to be picked by another crazy?"

"Exactly."

"But how do you know I'm not crazy as well."

His eyes took me in for a second. "Because you've been standing over her by yourself. You haven't engaged any of the waiters that I've seen and you aren't downing the drink like its water."

"Oh." I smiled and it was genuine. This man wasn't what I thought. He was nice and soft. Not demanding I give him an erection so he could fuck me. Hell, he was nicer than most of the guys I've bumped into on nights out. "Well they always say watch out for the quiet ones."

"Something tells me you're safe." And I smiled

again. "Something also tells me this is your first time. You seem quite nervous."

"Yeah, this is my first time doing anything like this. I was brought here by a friend."

"Maybe I could help point him out to you?"

"Don't you want me to save you from the crazies?"

His laugh somehow carried his accent with it. "It's okay. You seem to be needing more help than me right now. What's his name?"

"Matt?"

"Don't know him by name. They aren't usually exchanged at these parties. Anything else you can tell me about him?"

"Brown hair. Built just like the others here." I was about to mention the scar but figured this guy wasn't checking out the other guy's arses when getting changed. "Other than that I don't know anything that could help."

"I'll ask around."

"Thank you. And good luck in finding a nice, normal woman."

"Here's hoping." The tall man leant down and pecked my cheek before walking off into the crowd. He wasn't what I had been expecting and actually had me more relaxed now. Then my eyes moved across the action and I wondered if Matt had already been taken by one of these women who just wanted sex.

I sipped more of my drink as another waiter arrived in my presence. His hair was brown and the rest of the description matched what I had given to the grey waiter. "I hear you're looking for me."

"Matt?"

I looked up into his eyes. His voice had sounded off but that could be the mask he was wearing. It was covering everything apart from his eyes. "Yeah. How about you reach down and give me something to play with."

I thought about it but something just didn't seem right about him. So I stared into his eyes until a hand came down on his shoulder. The new waiter leant into his ear and whispered something I couldn't catch.

But whatever he said had the youngster running off quickly. And when I looked up at the new arrival I almost threw my arms around him. Looking into those eyes I knew it was him. He didn't have to speak or lift up that mask. It was Matt. I was certain of it.

And when he smiled it confirmed it. But there was no harm in double checking. "You know I heard a story about one of the waiters here." I stepped closer to him and pressed my middle fingertip to his abs. Licking my lips as I felt his muscles tense under my soft touch.

Circling around him my touch slid around his hip and tucked into the back of his boxers. Pulling them down I let my eyes take in those cheeks. They looked so good I wanted to just dig my teeth into them. Then I yanked them down further.

The right butt cheek was smooth and I could tell it would feel firm against my fingertips. But the left wasn't completely smooth. Almost right in the middle of it was an inch long scar.

Leaving his underwear down I ran my finger over that raised slit. Grinning as he squirmed a little. I giggled and looked up at him. His head turned to bring his eyes to mine.

Then his smooth voice moved to my ears. "Satisfied?"

"With many things. You'll have to tell me at some point how you got this scar. Jenny told me it has a very good story behind it."

His grin told me she had been right. "Why don't you come around the front? Might be something else you find satisfying."

"I know I find that part of you satisfying." But I did as he suggested. My fingertip still inside his underwear. Brushing across the base of him, feeling that softness. Cocking an eyebrow as I looked up at him. "Looks like I'm going to have to try harder."

Matt didn't answer or comment. He simply grinned down at me, his arm still holding up that tray of champagne. With all the thoughts running through my head I simply chose the simplest. Pulling out those shorts a little further before turning my wrist and pushing my hand against him.

Fingertips ran through his trimmed pubes before wrapping around his member. And the soft moan that he produced had me grinning. Not only that but my body reacted. Feeling an emptiness that needed filling. I slowly moved my hand. My stare burning into his as the lust built between us.

I fought the urge to just take him and decided to try and tease him. But as he grew against my touch I longed for it more. And he grew and grew. Reminding me just how thick he actually was. It got to the point where I had to pull down his underwear to give him more space.

As it popped free I let my eyes dip low and they widened when I saw it. Despite our previous fun it caught be by surprise again. Finding myself wondering how this monster fit inside me in the first place.

Looking up I bit my bottom lip. My hand moved up to his fat head. Running my thumb over it I felt his body squirming. "I have a question to ask you now. But make sure you think about it before answering."

"Okay." My breath was a whisper compared to his. It slightly annoyed me that he seemed so in control of himself. On the other side of the scale my knees were so weak they could give way at any moment.

"Slave or master?" His smile was full of mischief.

My lips moved ready to say master. Matt had been so much in control the last time we played. This time I wanted to be the one to take him. To tease him until his eyes pleaded for the frustration to end.

But when I locked eyes with him there was something deep down. His power and passion were so clear. Something that made me seem so small and inexperienced even though I wasn't. The word escaping my lips with a shiver of anticipation. "Slave."

Matt grinned wide. His fingers wrapped around my wrist and tugged my grip free from him.

I stood there, my breathing starting to become deeper as he tucked himself away. My forehead crinkled with confusion but that smile reassured me of his intentions. A hand came up to cradle my chin and I was pulled to his lips. I moaned as they touched and massaged over mine.

But it was sweet and sensual. Something I didn't expect from a master after watching the previous action. The kiss broke, his breath washing over my lips. My eyes opened to find him staring down at me. "I need to know before I do anything. That you give yourself to me completely. That I am free to do as I wish."

"I don't know. What do you have planned?"

"I can't tell you that. That would spoil the surprise." My lips parting as his thumb came to rub across them.

"I guess....." A small part of me was still screaming for me to run out of here. Only I was hooked. Needing to know what he had planned. Feeling so exposed in this room with everyone able to see us. Only it was like a different world. Once Matt had me, it was just me and him. "I trust you." Trusting this man I had only met a few days ago. I barely knew anything real about him and here I was. Giving my body to him, to any whim that popped inside his head. And yet, I felt safe.

"Then hopefully you will enjoy this."

"I'm sure I will." In my mind I just thought he

was going to fuck me right here in this room with everyone able to watch. That in itself was something I had never thought about doing and yet it had my arousal marking my knickers.

But when he turned away from me and took a few steps I wondered what he was thinking. There I was wearing a nice dress and feeling that urge deep down to have him take me. And here he was walking away. Making my forehead crease up in confusion.

I quickly tossed back the rest of my champagne. Breathing at a loss when my eyes landed on him again. My teeth digging into my lip as I saw the cuffs swinging from his finger. Leather rings attached together by a line of metal hoops. Big buckles tapped together with a soft clink as he moved them.

My eyes flicked to his face. Not only did I see that grin but I saw his idea swimming in his eyes. As he came back to me I looked around at the others in the room. Most of them were occupied in their own naughtiness but a few of them were watching us. Including Jenny who seemed very interested in what we would do. Turning back to Matt, the space between us had been devoured. This man was close enough to snap those things around my wrists.

So I retreated. Moving from the bar and around the piano with Matt following me. This little cat and mouse game had my breath catching. Despite the impending state of being locked and subdued with his toy I was smiling. That look on his face had my mind at ease and yet, my heart was racing.

Another step matched with Matt's until my

back hit the wall. I thought about skipping to the side but there I froze. Back flat on the cool wood and Matt coming closer and closer. His eyes burned into mine as I looked back. "What do you have planned?"

There was no answer. Matt knew what he was doing and his act of being the master had me wanting to find out. Feeling like a character in one of his books. His movements like sentences on a page.

Feeling myself chanting that safe-word in my head. Not wanting to forget it through the heat my body was creating. I wanted Matt and knowing he wanted me made it even hotter. And that look in his eyes had me knowing that he had naughty ideas. I had my own thoughts of what would happen but not knowing if I was right had me squirming against the wall. Pressing my thighs together.

Matt held out the handcuffs towards me, "Could you hold these for me?"

"Um... Sure." I whispered out the words just in case someone heard me. I took them and they felt heavier than they should. The two halves clinking together as they hung on my fingers by the chain.

Matt leant forward, lips brushing mine which had me gasping sharply. His laugh trickled out through his breathing. Then those hands of his slid to my shoulders. Palms running flat down against my arms. Sparking up electricity between us.

His fingers played with mine before they curled around my hips. Then he turned me slowly. My sight losing his face. Looking at the dark brown wood of the wall. The only information of the room were the noises of moans and orders from the masters. His touch briefly skimmed over my thighs.

Hiking my dress a little but then dropping it back down. Everything he did heightened my body. My nipples hardening against my bra. Wanting them to be touched. To be played with. Then my breath froze like a lump of ice in my throat as I felt the zip of the dress move. Slowly as each partner of teeth came apart.

Hot breath swam into my dress as it parted at the back. I shivered yet again, knowing that was exactly what he wanted. My zip hit the bottom of my spine. I covered my front up, worrying that my dress would just fall from me. A single fingertip touched between my shoulder blades. I arched my back as it trailed down, my arse sticking out.

Heat had my skin scorching where he touched. Then another breath hit my back making me push my breasts out even more and I found myself cupping them. Squeezing them softly. Moaning before I could stop myself.

Material slid over my shoulders and my dress loosened. Taking a deep breath before letting it go. The material skating down my body before pooling at my ankles. Revealing my underwear to everyone.

My cheeks hot as they flushed. The cool leather of the cuffs touched around my skin. Doing very little to scare away the heat Matt was creating. And that fire doubled when my bra straps were moved from my shoulders. The soft lacy material slipped and hung around my elbows.

I looked over my shoulder. The circles in his mask amplified that look he gave me and my knees almost buckled right there. "What's next?"

"Next, I take those off of you." He plucked the cuffs from me and I giggled.

"What are you going to do with them?"

"You are full of questions aren't you. Have you never heard of enjoying the moment?"

"I'm sorry. Just curious."

"No need to say sorry." Matt smiled, flashing those pearly teeth. "At Christmas, wasn't it better when you didn't know the presents you were about to receive?"

"Are you comparing yourself with Christmas?"

"I think I'll bring a smile to your face."

"I'm hoping you'll give me more than a smile."

"That's what I'm planning."

I just stared up at his eyes with those words coming from his kissable lips. But when I moved to kiss him, he backed away. And laughed that laugh that had my hormones bouncing around. "Remember, I'm the master. You're the slave."

"Sorry, sir." He seemed to like the fact I called him sir because he rewarded me with a soft kiss. As he pulled away my lips curled and I giggled.

"Just remember, you're the slave. Behave like one."

"Yes, sir. What do you want me to do?"

"Pull those arms out from your bra but don't remove it, yet." He held the straps out for me. I did what a good slave should do and followed his orders. Slipping my arms out, the clasp the only thing stopping my bra from dropping to the floor.

Then I was suddenly pulled back against him. His hard muscles and that hardness in his underwear pressed to me. So I rubbed back against it. Sliding my arse up and down, making him moan in response. My heart beat was pounding in my chest. I could feel my breast moving with it.

I heard a clink and then the feel of leather wrapping around my wrist. First the left, then the right. I pulled my arms apart and felt the tension between them. Cuffed and bound up for him which just made this whole thing even hotter. Surrendering my body to his thoughts.

Getting spun around. Taking a deep breath and letting it out. Feeling my bra slip a little lower. The fabric teasing my hard nipples. Sending tingles across my skin.

Then I felt his finger. Touching my neck and then sliding lower. Down over my collar bone and the swell of my breast. I couldn't stop the racing in my chest as it moved over the curve. Then to the cup of my bra.

We shared a heated glance before he pulled it down. As his eyes feasted on my bare flesh I pushed it out towards him. My nipple burning for attention. Lips parting as he moved and I felt his mouth wrapping around it. Sending a pulse of joy as it got what it wanted. Feeling his tongue flicking against it, making me arch more. Feeding him my curve before he sucked hard, a loud moan shooting from my mouth.

Twisting my hands, trying to break free from those cuffs so I could grab his head. Keep him there so this delicious feeling wouldn't stop. But I couldn't and Matt tugged his head back. My eyes dropped as it was released with a pop. My chest rising and falling, no words could describe my breathing.

Rapid was too slow. Heavy didn't work. Ragged wasn't right. And it was all Matt's doing. The whole room around us had disappeared and it was only him I could see. Breathing in sharply as I felt his fingertip touching me again.

It curved over my chest, my whole body arching. The other cup being slipped off my nipple. Closing my eyes, wishing to feel his mouth again. The ache beyond bearable as I waited. Seconds stretching out for so long. Mouth open and poised ready to breath in with that pleasure.

Then a pinch hit my nipple which produced a surprised yelp like noise. His fingertips twisted and pulled. All this torture had my knickers drenched. Squeezing my thighs together so tightly, rubbing them back and forth. So ready for him he could have thrust so easily inside me right now.

But he didn't. He simply let go of my nipple and stood there, looking at them as they poked out over my bra. Feeling his body grow closer, the soft cling of metal as one of those cuffs was opened.

The release making me miss that tightness over my skin. My arms being moved in front of me. Tip-toeing up to him as he bound them back together.

His voice coming steady, filled with authority. "Such a good girl."

"Thank you, master." Smiling as I felt that rush between us.

Matt hooked a finger under the chain linking my wrists together and moved them high above my head. Making my breasts slip further out of my bra turning it into a useless piece of material around my ribs. I heard metal on metal and I watched his hands slide down from mine.

Skating across my skin until his hands rested around my sides. Feeling so exposed which just made me love it even more. Pulling on my arms to touch him but they snagged against something. My head shot up. Seeing my cuffs hooked over a light fixing.

I shot a glare back at Matt. His body lightly pressed to mine. The heat from his chest burned on my nipples making them ache even more. My thighs squirmed together as he purposefully swayed from left to right. Dragging his skin against mine. "Don't forget the safe word but god, please don't use it."

It was the only chance I had to tease him back. "Ballo......."

His eyes widened as I giggled. "You'll pay for that, little lady." His next move was filled with speed. Fingers moved around my ribs and unclasped my bra.

Then he dropped to a knee. I didn't watch, instead shutting my eyes. Feeling fingers curl into my knickers before they were yanked down. The cool air of the room feeling completely opposite to the heat I felt. A shiver ran from my head to my toes when I felt his breath kissing my mound. Knowing he could see the arousal marking my lips.

Then his mouth pursed to me. And I moaned so loud it drowned out the beating of my own heart. Pushing forwards, making his touch part my lips. Wanting him to taste me and feel what he was doing to me.

But his lips were gone just as quick as they had come. Everything he was doing was to tease and torture me and I was annoyed that it was working so well. My eyes still shut his lips pressed to mine. His tongue snaking in slowly. Tasting my sweetness. And to my surprise it turned me on even more.

All these sensations pushing me to kiss him harder. The cuffs snapping against the light. Making me press towards him so needy. Wanting to hold him close and just feel him inside me.

Only once again, Matt pulled back. And I swore at him as he kept moving. Slowly walking away just like he had for the cuffs. Watching his arse sway in his tight underwear. Cursing that he hadn't removed them yet. My body was begging for pleasure. To be satisfied. Instead it was being tortured and what made it even more annoying was how good it felt.

He turned back to me, holding a long feather in his fingers. It was swung from left to right as he stalked towards his prey. I saw the devil in his grin. The feather was brought closer until the soft tip of it hit my neck. Drawing down over goose bumped skin. Such a soft, gentle touch. Making my nipple tingle as it passed over it.

Deep sucks of breath filled my lungs. Trying to regain control of it but every time that feather shifted across my skin, I gasped again. And again. Feeling the tip flutter in and out of my naval. Dipping down over me, feeling it stick as it touched against my arousal. The noises of the room, no matter how loud, were just lost to what I was experiencing. All I could think about was Matt and what he was doing to me.

My whole body was on fire for him and I could feel that heat dribbling down my thigh. I blinked and it felt like minutes before they opened again. Speaking with a whisper, "You either fuck me right now or I'll say the safe word and finish myself off." Not able to pull a smile. Breathless and so needy.

The feather was put down and my heart skipped a beat when he removed his boxers. His meat was still rock hard and the head was covered in his pre-cum. So much that it dribbled from his head and down his shaft.

Dragging my right foot up against the wall. Then spreading it out wide, opening myself to him. His eyes dipped then shot back to mine. Feeling his body press. Tits to his chest. My leg hooking around him, pulling him closer.

Then the exquisite touch of his wet head on my lips. Parting as it was rubbed up and down. Then, that push. That deliberately slow push inside. Biting my bottom lip, heading swinging back so hard it hit the wall. Groaning out like an animal as his rock hard length impaled me. Pushing all the way in, hitting balls deep. My moan escaping loudly at the fullness of that feeling.

I reached up and grabbed hold of the light. Using my leg around his waist to pull him in as I bucked my hips. After all that teasing, I wanted nothing but pure pleasure. One constant rhythm As our bodies slapped together. Feeling him thrust and my back hitting the wall each time.

His cock head rubbing so deep inside me. I was helpless against his ravaging and I loved being his slave. Loved it all as I moaned and groaned. Telling him how much I was enjoying his cock. Telling the whole room how much I loved him fucking me in front of them.

A hand cupping my other thigh and I was pulled into the air. Pressed to the wall to be taken even harder. Each thrust bursting noise from my mouth. Massaging his thick inches between clenched walls. Arching and rolling my hips. Trying to get every part of my body on his. The burning of my muscles was nothing. Barely feeling it at all as we moved.

Long thrusts of power sending my mind crazy, wild. My head spinning with the orgasm that was threatening to rip my whole world apart. Gasping, trying to make sense of everything I felt. Until my breath caught and the orgasm rippled through every fibre of my being and I screamed out. One long noise as he kept fucking me. Kept that feeling of pure bliss rocking my body. The sloppy sounds of the mess he was creating joining in with the applause.

That drawn out orgasm making him glide so easily even as I clenched. Feeling his hips getting

BARTOND

quicker, more urgent. Then those wet shots hit deep inside me. Hearing his grunts as he used my body to unload.

Capping my orgasm with the feeling of his hitting so deep. Taking all he was offering and wanting every last drop of it as I clenched down on him. Milking him as he draw himself in and out.

When I thought I was about to pass out he pressed and held inside me. My sex was filled to the brim and it brought a rude grin to my lips. And we held ourselves there against the wall. Me clinging to him with my legs and his body pressed to mine. Such a blissful moment.

I pressed my forehead against his shoulder. That's when my eyes looked out over the room. Only a few of them were still playing with each other. The rest including the two hosts of the party were staring at us. Some with slacked jaws and the rest with stupidly big grins.

The sudden eruption of applause made me jump against his sweaty skin. But then I gave out a giggle as my cheeks filled with red embarrassment. And that's when Matt pulled out of me. The sudden vacancy had me wanting to cover up.

Luckily Matt popped open the cuffs and I quickly grabbed my dress, kissed Matt on the cheek and jogged out of the room with a massive grin. I got to the hallway and my legs suddenly gave way. After sex jelly legs hit me hard and I only stopped myself hitting the floor because I grabbed the table in front of me.

I turned and perched myself on the edge. My breathing coming in quick shots of air as my eyes peered up to the double doors. Jenny came walking through them and shut them behind where I saw a glimpse of Matt getting dressed. He looked just as happy as I felt.

The host came over to me with a worried look on her face. "You okay, sweetie?"

I let out a breathless giggle. "Yeah. My body feels amazing. Just a little embarrassed that I actually did that. Or rather, had that done to me."

"Matt did look like he was enjoying himself. He wasn't the only one." She came forwards and took my dress from my reluctant hands. I was surprised when she knelt and slipped it up my legs.

I moved away from the table, using her shoulders to steady myself and allowed her to dress me. Covering my modesty up which I was grateful for. When she stood her lips pulled back in a big smile and I smiled back.

She turned me around and the zip was pulled up. "You know, for an innocent, you are a lot of fun. I hope you decide to come again in the future."

"I don't know." Then I thought about the feeling I got with all those people watching me with Matt. "Maybe. Have to wait and see."

"Well, each party is different. And of course, you don't always have to participate."

"I really will think about it. Really." Turning around and giving her a friendly smile.

"You should. Go take five minutes outside. You

look like you could us some fresh air."

Smiling I did as I was told. On the way out I grabbed Matt's keys from their hook. Thinking of slipping into his leather seat with the window open. So exhausted mentally I would probably drift off for a nap.

Then breeze hit my skin, cooling it, filling my lungs as I breathed it in. My feet scrunched as I stepped over the gravel drive way. Shooting pain up my legs. I couldn't even remember when my shoes had been slipped off my brain was so occupied.

Instead of climbing in I slid myself onto the bonnet, stepping my feet onto the bumper. The night sky just looked like a blanket of black. No stars were visible and the moon must have been hiding behind the large house.

The sound of gravel grinding underneath footsteps had me looking. Expecting to see Matt wearing a stupid grin but instead I saw a blonde watching me. I hadn't seen her in the room and she wasn't wearing a mask.

Which meant I could recognise her from the hospital. She had been the one I saw talking to Matt. Swallowing past the lump in my throat. "Hi."

"Hey, special girl. Hell of a show you put on in there."

"Not really. It was mostly Matt."

"Well anyone with eyes could see that. My compliment wasn't aimed at you. Just making one in general."

"Okay." I looked away. Trying to pretend I saw

something in the distance that interested me.

"Can't believe he brought you here."

"I beg your pardon?" Something inside me bit back sharply.

"Well, this was our thing. Our parties. I was his woman to parade around in front of his friends."

"Weren't you in there anyway?"

"No. I didn't get the invite this time." My eyes took in the red dress she wore. It was so elegant but if she hadn't been in the party, why was she wearing it? "Do you even know Matt well enough to come to a strange place in the middle of nowhere? Is that wise?"

I tried to ignore her but why the hell was she here. I needed to find out what her problem was. "I think I know Matt pretty well."

"Because you've fucked? In that case half the women in the city know him pretty well. Me included."

"What is your problem? Are you jealous?"

"When you're jealous of someone. It means you're afraid of that person taking something that is yours. You aren't taking anything from me. He'll be done with you just like the many others before you. He always comes back. It's only a matter of time. It's always been me and his wife. Now she's died I'm the only one left in his heart."

"If you're trying to shock me it's not going to work. Matt already told me about his ex-wife." He had mentioned her problem with drinking but nothing more.

"I suppose having your wife die makes her an

ex-wife. But it's only been a few days."

I almost fell from the car. "What?"

"Who do you think he was visiting in the hospital that day?"

"His sister." I wanted to slide from the bonnet but the gravel would dig into my soles. "He was lying to me?"

"Are you at all shocked? He's a writer. Quick at thinking on his feet. Anything to get you in the sack I imagine."

The pain that struck my heart was like being hit by a bolt of lightning. It took my breath away. And when I saw Matt come walking out through the mirrored doors it got worse. That person had spun his little lies to get my clothes off. To fuck me and now he had done it in front of his friends. Shown me off and shown the control he had over me. Just like the others. I was nothing more than a number in his mind.

But not any more. My eyes met his and then he looked at the blonde. His face dropped and filled with the horror of what she must be telling me. He leapt down the steps that led up to the house and ran over to me.

But he wasn't quick enough. I unlocked the car and slid into the front seat. My foot stung with pain as a stone dug into my skin as I slammed on the accelerator. Matt was yelling something at me but my ears were shut off to his lies now.

Tears stung my eyes and poured down my cheeks as I roared onto the main road and headed off into the city. There was no way I could head home. The lack of Kelly made the place seem empty as it was. All I would do is sit there and cry about how silly I had been. Just when I was starting to feel something for Matt more than the desire and lust that he brewed in my heart.

Driving around the city was a stupid idea. My eyesight was already blurry from my crying and I couldn't stop myself. They just kept coming and coming making me run a very blurred red light. The honks of other cars scared the hell out of me.

So I went to the one place I had been spending most of my time anyway. Parking the car and not caring if he got a ticket. Wearing this elegant dress had me sticking out like a sore thumb. Turning heads as I made my way through the hallways. Bursting into my daughter's room before anyone else could see me.

The door hit shut against the door frame hard. My back was pushed against it and I slowly slipped down to the ground. That's when the tears truly fell. Covering my face in them as I shut my eyes and tried to forget the pain that killed my heart.

And there I stayed for as long as I was awake. I wasn't really tired but the pain wore me down quickly and that's why I fell asleep.

Chapter 7

I woke to the feeling of warmth and security.
Like the horrible world that I had left behind when
I slept was a mere memory. My ears picked up the
beeping of my daughter's machine. The smell of the
hospital floated up my nose and awoke my other
senses.

The one thing that didn't belong was the
rhythmic breathing of someone else in the room.
Someone so close I could smell his aftershave.
Opening my eyes I saw the blue shirt and the dark
blue tie right in front of my eyes. I shuffled my body
trying to get up but fingers slipped through my hair.
Combing down to the tips where they brushed my
bare shoulders.

"You look beautiful."

Clearing my throat I whispered back, "Thanks."
I felt his body tensing next to me as he sat up. "How
long have you been here?"

"Long enough to get some sleep. Definitely
have to nip to the shower before my next shift
though."

"When is that?"

"In thirty minutes."

"What?" That made me sit up from his chest. Looking into those cute eyes. The depths of sweetness in them had me smiling. "You really are a great man."

He showed me those white teeth of his and that killer smile. "You're sweet when you've just woken up."

"I know I've been a bit of a bitch lately."

"Don't mention it. I've forgotten about it."

"I have something to tell you. I want you to know everything if we're going to make this work."

"I'm not going to like this am I?"

"Absolutely not." I laughed nervously. But when I looked into his eyes I felt a little at ease. Like even though he would get angry, he would forgive me. He would understand how we weren't exclusive. And at least I could tell him that whatever me and Matt had, was now over.

So I told him everything. How I met Matt and everything that followed. Even went into detail about the party which just came blurting out once I got going. The doctor sat there, looking into my eyes the whole time. Taking in the information I gave him.

By the time I was finished, he didn't even have enough time to shower before his shift started. So when we stood I grabbed his arm. "Say something?"

Greg turned to me and smiled and it was a genuinely sweet smile. No anger or anything evident in his look. "We're good. I'll be back later. To check on you both."

I was over-whelmed by how he took it so easily and I cried again. And Greg pulled me into a tight hug which didn't stop my tears.

Just his action of sleeping here with me had me feeling the warmth in my heart. Then how he reacted to what I'd been up to. Greg was the one to hold onto. The sweet guy who would look after me. My eyes were wide open to this now.

And the difference between him and Matt was like comparing a mountain to a mole-hill. Knowing I had to leave that writer behind and all that came along with him. To move on with Greg.

With the room now left with the beep of the machine and nothing else. I sat down in my usual spot, feeling silly still in the dress that wasn't even mine. There was no doubt I would have to go back and return it to Kelly's wardrobe.

Typically I would have grabbed a book and read. Pass the time with my daughter. Spending what was now classed as quality time with her. But instead I went back to sleep. Staying awake was still too painful and I was tired enough to slip into dreamland where everything seemed so much better.

But we all had to wake up at some point. When I did, real life had gotten worse somehow. Sitting on the opposite side of the room was Matt. Wearing the same stuff he wore last night.

When he noticed me stirring he placed one of my books on his knee. Then he smiled. Before it would have had my hormones bouncing around but instead, it now had my skin crawling. Turning away from him. "Get out."

"But I came to explain."

Shooting out of my seat I walked over and grabbed the front of his t-shirt. Pulling him out of the seat was beyond my power but I yanked anyway. Ordering him to get out once again. "This is my daughter's room. Before you came here this was my sanctum. A place where I could come and the outside world couldn't touch me. Now it's ruined with your lies and stink."

"But..." I slapped his words out of his mouth with my hand.

"Get out of here. I don't want to know what lies you have to tell. I just want you out of my life."

Matt stood up out of his seat and went to the door. As he turned I prepared my hand for another slap despite my palm stinging like hell already. "Sorry." I didn't slap him but I turned my back on him.

Walking to look at my daughter there in her bed. Eyelids shut like she was sleeping. And I thought that just for a moment. Something I never let myself do. Always making sure I reminded myself that it was a coma. That it was unlikely that she would ever wake up.

But right now I needed some form of hope. Something to hold onto just to bring my life up a notch. A little glimmer of sunshine. Until I heard the door of the room open and shut with a soft thud.

The sound of wood hitting wood was like a signal for my tears to start pouring. Liquid covering my cheeks and dripping down onto the bed. My fingers rubbed the marks but they wouldn't come off. Like permanent stains on this place. Something left behind by Matt's horrible lies.

I pulled the cover off of her and chucked it into the corner. She had been here long enough for me to know where everything was kept. So I replaced it and just left the marked one on the floor. Discarded. Something I wish I could do with my memories involving Matt.

With my daughter clean I occupied my chair, staring at the wall. Not reading or paying much attention to anything in the room or anything outside the room. Just staring into space. There wasn't even a part of my brain that noticed when I started feeling tired. Just when the darkness quickly came flooding into my thoughts.

Just like the last time I awoke in this room, in this dress. There were others with me. One of them was Greg but the other I didn't recognise. So I quickly rubbed the drool from my chin and stood up. Smoothing out my dress I felt a little more presentable. "Hey, Greg. Who's this?"

Greg brought his thumb up to my chin and wiped off a spot of spit I had missed. "I want you to me a specialist doctor. This is Doctor Miller."

"Nice to meet you." I shook his hand none the wiser. "I don't mean to be rude but what are you doing here? I mean, in my daughter's room."

His voice came out deep from behind that bushy beard. "I thought you would have been told."

"About?" Eye switching between the two doctors.

Greg touched my arm. "Just listen to what the

doctor has to say."

My attention flicked to Doctor Miller. "Will one of you just tell me what's going on?"

"Take a seat, please." I did so as his eyes looked at my dress. "You look very smart."

"Thanks." I didn't know what his comment was about but I had no patience to decipher it.

"I've been experimenting with some brain chemical manipulation. I don't think there's any point in going into the specifics with you. I don't mean to sound rude but it gets very technical."

"Please, Greg here knows I don't do the talk."

"Good. So I will put it like this. What I can do is open up your daughter's skull."

"What!" I was so surprised by his statement that I shot up out of my chair. "You're not cracking open my daughter's head and poking around. What is this? To see how the brain works when someone is in a coma? That's barbaric."

Greg touched my shoulder. "Actually he has a way of waking her from the coma."

What Greg said hit me like a sledgehammer and my legs almost gave way. "What are you talking about?" My breath holding in my throat, holding with that sudden glimmer of hope.

"If you would let me continue." The doctor took his glasses off and started cleaning them on his tie. "I will open up her skull, yes. But I will not be probing or cutting into her brain. It's a simple application of liquids and chemicals that will interact with what is already there. Something like kick starting a car engine."

"And she'll wake up?"

"It's a small chance that it'll work."

"How small?"

"Just over twenty percent."

"And what happens if it doesn't work?"

"There is a possibility that she will never wake up after this procedure. She could turn into a vegetable. And an even smaller chance, she could die from the procedure."

"Die?" The doctor slowly nodded in response. My eyes filled up with tears as I turned to the vulnerable girl in her bed. I couldn't lose her but then, I didn't really have her right now. I hadn't had a conversation with her in such a long time. It's been too long since I had seen her smile.

I knew it was the recent events that pushed me into saying yes but I lied to myself. Told myself that it was my decision and that it was a good idea. An excellent idea that would bring me back, face to face with the angel that I lost.

"Do it? How soon can you perform it?"

"I can have my team and my equipment here within a couple of hours."

"That all sounds very expensive." My heart already sinking. Knowing that I had spent all my savings, plus what I got from selling my home. The little that I had left was spent on keeping my daughter here in the first place.

"The bill has already been taken care of."

"Oh?" Looking at Greg but he seemed just as

surprised as I was. "By who?"

"It was anonymous."

My interest pushing me to question further. "How did you hear about my daughter's condition?"

"An anonymous benefactor to my research. Do you have any more questions or do I have your consent to go ahead?"

"Yes, please."

"Excellent. I'll leave all the extra information with Doctor Greg for you to go through." The older doctor left the room, digging his phone out of his pocket as he went.

I turned to Greg. Speaking but my mind was occupied with something else. "What extra information?"

"It's just consent forms. Typical lawyer stuff to keep the hospital and doctor's from being sued."

"If something should go wrong." Looking at my daughter. My fingers curling into hers. "Do you think this is a bad idea?"

"There hasn't been any sign of her waking up the whole time she's been here. It's not my position to speak. Not as your doctor or even your friend. This is your decision."

"But if I asked for your opinion?" Moving my body close to his, hugging him tightly.

"I would want to speak to my daughter, to see her grow up. You can't do that whilst she lays here in this bed. And she may never wake up. At least this way, you have a chance."

"Thank you." Closing my eyes, hearing his

words as confirmation it was the right decision. Pulling away. "You've got a job to do. But will I see you before she goes in?"

"Yes you will. I'll drop off the forms in a little bit and Doctor Miller is allowing me to assist with the surgery. So I will be in the room with her the whole time."

"That makes me feel a little more at ease." Looking up into his eyes. "And us?"

"Louise. Let's put us on hold for now. Until after this operation. This could change your life for the better....or worse. When you know which, we can discuss us. Sound good?"

"As good as can be. I'll see you later." Greg left the room. Leaving me with my wonder and thoughts. Wondering who would have got Doctor Miller involved but there was really only one person who would do it. One person with the money to be an anonymous benefactor.

The writer who had broken my heart. Trying to buy his way back into my life. Using my daughter to do it. I would take this operation and the results that came with it. But I wasn't about to let him back in because of it.

The next hour went by in a blur. Signing forms and being told in greater detail what would happen. The possible side-effects short and long term. All the information going in one ear and out the other because all I could think about was my decision. Had it been the right one? Did I just kill my daughter?

The moment coming when they came in to

take her away. Doctor Miller came over to me. "I will take care of your daughter. I've been studying her medical records for a couple of days now."

"A couple of days?"

"Yes. She was brought to my attention on Monday. I've been studying her coma ever since."

"But." My mind hit with a grenade. Matt had brought this doctor into my daughter's life before last night. Before we fucked at Marie's.

"It's okay, she's in good hands."

"Thank you, doctor. I don't like getting my hopes up. But.."

"Sometimes it's what we need. To look on the brighter side of life and all the possibilities it can possess."

"Yes." Smiling, feeling a tear trickle down my cheek.

"We best get her going."

"Okay." I leant over my little girl and kissed her forehead. Telling myself that next time it happens, she'll smile up at me. I will exchange words with her and make her laugh. Feeling my heart fluttering with the hope.

Then she was wheeled out of the room. Leaving me alone. I thought about going to see Kelly but then I would have to explain what was going on. Right now I just wanted to grasp that hope and never let it go.

So I sat in the chair. Opened up one of my books. Trying to read but finding I went over the same paragraph five times. Leaning back and shutting my eyes. Drifting off thinking about watching my daughter grow old. Getting her first job and her first love. Sleep taking me on a boat ride of what could be. Drifting along with a smile.

Chapter 8

Finding myself stirring in my sleep. My dress clinging to my body as I sat up. Feeling the chair cradling my body just like it always did. Only something was off. There was no steady rhythmic beep of a machine.

I opened my eyes and looked over to the bed. My heart sinking as the thing was empty. No daughter laying there. My whole body feeling like it was about to be swollen by the emptiness growing.

I shot to the door and yanked it open. Seeing the nurse sitting at the station. Taking a deep breath before speaking. "The bed. It's empty. My daughter."

She quickly climbed to her feet and came around to pull me into a hug. "It's okay. There's nothing wrong. She's out of surgery. She's been moved to be kept an eye on."

"What?" My brain refusing to comprehend her words. The worry still filling my brain. "Where is she?"

"I'll take you to her. It's okay." She curled an arm around my body. Feeling like I was hovering across the floor. The hospital moving around me. The hallway giving way to one of the wards. Seeing curtains pulled for privacy.

Empty beds sitting there waiting for occupancy. Then my eyes hit her. My daughter. Laying in a new bed. That beep coming intermittently. The feeding tube still in her mouth. Seeming like nothing had changed.

But the doctors. They were smiling. Doctor Miller getting taps on the back and handshakes from others. My feet took over and I crossed the ward. Grabbing Greg and spinning him around. "What happened?"

"It's great news. She's become responsive."

"Responsive." My brain delved into all the research I had done when this first happened. "That's good."

"Very good."

A smile breaking through the sorrow. Happiness filling my heart. Pushing that hope back to the front of my brain. "So, this is the first step towards.."

"That's very likely." The deep voice of Doctor Miller had me stepping towards him. "It still may take some time. But I'm extremely positive that your daughter will wake."

"Do you know when?" My voice shaky. "Can you tell me when you think she will?"

"Judging by how well she has responded to the procedure already. Using other experiments as reference. Maybe a week or two."

"Oh my god." I lifted a hand to my mouth. Feeling it shake in shock.

"She will obviously need further recovery time after being in a coma for so long. But you should be looking forward to getting your daughter back."

"Thank you so much." Leaping into a hug. Pulling the doctor close. "Thank you, thank you."

"It's my pleasure. I will be by every day to check on her progress, document with your permission."

"Yes, of course. Anything." Pulling back and wiping the tears of joy.

Greg came over to me as the doctor made his way out of the ward. "This is great news."

"Amazing." Eyes taking in my daughter as she laid there. Seeing the bandages wrapped around her head. "She will have a scar?"

"Yes but it was made at the side. The hair won't grow back there, but it will be very easy to cover it up."

"Great. Everything is just great." A moment of silence surrounded me as I watched her.

Greg's hand on my shoulder turned me towards him. "You should go home. Shower, change your clothes." His eyes running over the dress I still wore. "I'll get that horrible seat from the other room down here for you. I assume you'll be staying the night here instead?"

"Definitely. I want to be here when she wakes up. I don't want to miss a second."

"Alright but first. That shower." Nodding to his words. Not even wanting to make a joke about me smelling bad. Just beyond happy that she would be alright. Taking a while to drag myself away from her side.

Heading home and showering, getting myself into some proper clothes. Once cleaned I opened up the huge duffel bag I kept in the closet. It had been so long since it had been opened.

Looking inside and seeing my daughter's clothes. Pieces I had put away because it was too hard to see it hanging up. Grabbing a backpack and putting a few select items inside. Feeling myself getting happier as I went. Thinking about seeing her dressed in them. Walking around the hospital instead of being in that bed. Being dressed in a hospital gown.

Heading straight back to the hospital with that bag and a new outlook on life. Smiling as I saw that old chair sitting beside my daughter's new bed. Parking myself in my new home. Sitting right next to my sweet girl.

Epilogue

Ten days had passed. Sitting in that chair, sleeping through the night by her side. Reading my books and newspapers. Starting to plan for the future. Looking for a cheap two-bed apartment to rent. Even looking at new jobs since the one at the library wasn't paying me enough. My whole life was changing.

Doctor Miller had been coming around twice a day. Checking her response levels. Happy that her progress was moving forward and speeding up. He was saying that any day now could be the one.

My happiness had come back in full force. Brightening my personality, walking with a little skip in my step. That increased when I heard Kelly's voice. "Hey. How is she doing today?"

Folding my newspaper and placing it on the table next to me. "Her progress is still moving forward."

"That's good."

"It really is. He said any day she could be opening her eyes."

"I'm so happy for you."

"Thanks." I stood and gave her a tight hug. Feeling something poking me in the ribs. "What's this?"

"It was left at the apartment. Addressed to you."

"For me?" I pulled the thick envelope from her hand. "What is it?"

"I generally keep my x-ray vision for fighting crime. Sorry." I whacked her arm with the package. She winced through the pain it brought. "Sorry."

"I best get going to physical therapy. I'll stop by after."

"See you then." Giving her another hug before she walked out of the ward. I sat down. Fingers gripping the envelope and giving it a tug. One side coming away suddenly. A piece of paper fell to the floor. Placing the half-opened package on the table and plucking up what had fallen.

Flipping it open, spotting the name at the bottom. Biting my lip as I thought about the writer. Taking a deep breath before moving my eyes to the top and reading down.

Dear Louise, I know what you were told. Last time we chatted, I didn't get much time to explain. Yes, I was visiting my ex-wife at the hospital that day. We hadn't been together in a long time. But she contacted me because her life was coming to an end. The drink had finally got her and she wanted to see me before she died.

It was a long story that I didn't feel like sharing with a stranger. The sister thing just popped out and I thought that would be it. But then I got to know you and find out about your life and who you are deep down.

I didn't expect things to happen the way it did. But it has and I can't be sorry for that. Because you made me realise that I don't have to be shut off. That I can lower my walls to people.

You are amazing and I hope you have the perfect life. You deserve all the happiness you can get. With love, Matt.

P.S. check out the dedication.

Feeling my eyes welling, blinking those tears away quickly. Folding the letter up and placing it on the table. Lifting the package up and shifting the rest of the envelope away. Seeing that it was a printed off manuscript.

Seeing the title and Matt's pen name. The final part of the trilogy. I flicked over the first page and found the dedication. Smiling as I read it.

I dedicate this book to Louise. A woman who made me feel things I hadn't for a long time. Someone who showed me that it's okay to let people in. She made me smile and laugh. And truly made me feel that I had someone in my life that cared about me.

She was the only person that I've met in the last ten years that I can say with all my heart, was a true friend. The only person I could be myself with. It truly blessed my life bumping into her.

I'm ashamed to admit that I messed things up. Lost her but I will never make that mistake again if someone of worth pops into my life again. And I hope she gets her happy ending.

Taking a deep breath as I finished. Looking at

the manuscript. A sweet, thoughtful gift from a guy who might no be as bad as I first thought. He had his flaws but who doesn't. Thinking about getting in contact with him. Maybe becoming friends was plausible for our future.

Taking another deep breath, placing the wad of paper on the table. About to take a seat when I heard movement. A sigh and a shuffle. Turning slowly at the body on the bed. Watching as eyes opened that hadn't opened in almost a year.

My heart beating so fast. My bottom lip quivering. So close to crying. Then she spoke, in a soft, weak voice. But it was still hers. "Mum?"

Books By This Author

Moonlit Blood

Sunlit Blood

Burning Blood

Drowning Blood

Dead Blood

The Leecher Chronicles involves all things supernatural. From vampires and werewolves to witches and shifters. With reviews that mention it's originality and great characters. If you love anything supernatural, give this series a go.

Shadows In The Light

If you like a gritty take on superheroes then this

book is for you. Featuring heroes and villains and a storyline that will keep you gripped till the last page.

Crystal Darke

Crsytal Darke takes inspiration from Japanese Mythology. Imagine mashing Harry Potter and Pokemon together with influences from RPG fantasy games.